THE CLOWN ASSEMBLY

When the Horse Arrived

E.J. WADE

The characters in this book are a work of fiction and satire. This book contains dark comedy and at times may seem dramatic or scary. This is not a political partisan story that chooses sides, rather a careful examination of modern American Political systems.

ISBN:979-8-234-01717-8

Editor: E.J. Wade

Publisher: Mr. Wade Media, an independent media company

Manufactured in the United States

Library of Congress

The Clown Assembly: When the Horse Arrived

Mr. Wade holds an associate's degree in criminology and a bachelor's degree in interdisciplinary studies. He is also a veteran of the U.S. Navy. Mr. Wade is a former USCIS Immigration Services Officer and worked in the Special Immigrant Juvenile unit, as well as conducting over 4,000 interviews in the Field.

Mr. Wade is an active participant in the Books to Prisoners program in the state of Florida. He is a former member of The Most Worshipful Union Grand Lodge of Freemasons, Holy Royal Arch Masons and Ancient Order of Nobles Mystic Shrine.

Warning: This book contains adult language and situations and is not recommended for anyone under the age of 18.

Contact: Officialejwadepromo@gmail.com

Celebrating 250 Years of America

1776-2026

250

Table of Contents

ACT ONE

THE KINGMAKER

Ryan Flowergarden drives to a new restaurant to meet up with his boss. The "hip" political crowd eats there on Tuesdays. Ethan Sipper was a known kingmaker but was searching for his next star after losing for six years. Ryan walks through the double doors. He can smell the buttered toast and meat cooking in the back. He bumps into a waitress, who apologizes with her thick Southern accent.

Ryan finally arrives at the table to greet Ethan. Ethan is a large man with no "filter" on his language. He is often grumpy.

"Hey! Why would you bring me the eggs by themselves? Half of my breakfast is going to be hot and the other half cold. Where the fuck are you from?" Ethan yells at the new waitress.

The young lady is nervous as she apologizes.

"Bring me fresh, hot eggs with my meal!" Ethan says.

Ryan Flowergarden takes a seat in front of his boss.

"I found your next star," Ryan says.

Ethan looks at the packet Ryan handed him.

"Why and how?" Ethan asks.

"She is a commonsense moderate with a degree from Harvard. I went to Harvard with her," Ryan says.

Ethan hands the packet back to Ryan.

"I knew you would do this. You never trust me," Ryan says.

"No, I don't trust you. You didn't mention you're still fucking her!" Ethan yells.

Ryan looks around with embarrassment on his face.

"You didn't think I knew? I knew her father, Ryan," Ethan says as he stares into Ryan's eyes with fire.

"You have lost the last three races, and I stood by your side" Ryan shoots back, but he is interrupted.

"I paid you. As a matter of fact, I still pay you. So what you are going to do is stop complaining, come with me, and I will introduce you to our new star," Ethan says.

The two men stand as Ethan throws money on the table. The waitress comes out as they walk away.

"Sir, I have your hot breakfast!" she yells.

Without looking in her direction, Ethan yells back, "Fuck those eggs."

The two men get into an older black SUV with tinted windows and a personal driver.

"Did your star go to college?" Ryan asks.

Ethan ignores him as they continue driving. Eventually, the SUV pulls up to a park. A young lady wearing an Army shirt jogs by the men.

"You got Veronica Moorchester. How? She doesn't even like liberals," Ryan says.

"She is not doing this for us. She is doing it to save America," Ethan says.

Veronica walks up to the two men with a towel on her shoulder.

"Ms. Moorchester, my name is Ryan, and I am going to help you get elected," he says as he tries to shake her hand.

Veronica ignores his hand.

"Give me the strategy you were going to give your girlfriend. I expect it on my desk by Monday," she says.

She is a tall Samoan woman with legs the size of tree trunks and dark curly hair. Ryan nods, and she walks away without saying hello to Ethan. There is obvious tension between the two, but Ryan keeps quiet about it in her presence.

"Do you want to tell me why she has such a bad attitude?" Ryan asks.

"She hates liberals, and she hates us. But you will put her in office," Ethan says.

Ryan watches as she walks away.

"What will happen when we put a woman who hates us in office?" Ryan asks.

Ethan just looks at Ryan without a response.

"Get her the game plan by Monday. Do not be late," Ethan says.

"Anything else, boss?" Ryan says, anger in his voice.

"No, I want some breakfast now. Kid, you want something?" asks Ethan.

. Ryan just looks at Ethan with a straight face. On the inside, he wanted to rip Ethans head off his shoulders and yell down his neck.

Brenda Flowergarden brings Mavin Prep some coffee as he works on his artificial intelligence.

"Do you realize, with this invention, I will be able to put half of America out of work?" Mavin says.

"I think it's brilliant, but I can't help but think about the negatives," Brenda replies.

"If we really believe scarcity is right, then we need fewer humans. Resources on the planet are limited. If your job can be easily automated away, then it is natural selection," Mavin says.

Brenda looks sad.

"Hey, just continue your great work with data. Leave the A.I. stuff to me. The hard work must be done by somebody," Mavin says.

Brenda rolls her eyes, often offended by Mavin's remarks. He wears the exact same outfit every day so that he doesn't waste brain power on simple decisions.

Mavin pulls up a clone of himself.

"Clone Mavin, order us a pizza," he requests.

The clone inputs data online to order a pizza without touching any keyboards.

"Brenda, you're welcome to stay for some cheese pizza," Mavin says.

Brenda thinks about it but decides to skip dinner because she has a family meeting. Mavin always eats cheese pizza on Tuesday, once again so that he does not waste brain power deciding dinner every day. He is also constipated every Wednesday from too much cheese.

Brenda drives to her father's home on the outskirts of Atlanta. Her father opens the door and greets her. Brenda walks into the living room, where other members of the family are frowning at her. Her father, the rock of the family, looks disappointed.

"Honey, your brother told me you are working with that artificial intelligence devil stuff. Can't you see it is the antichrist?" Mr. Flowergarden says.

"You know what? Fuck this. Ryan is jealous of my career because I make more money than he does," Brenda yells.

Mr. Flowergarden attempts to calm her by giving her a hug.

"No!" she yells.

Ryan stands up.

"You just stand there with your smug, stupid look after trying to end my career?" Brenda yells.

A family member tries to touch Brenda's arm for comfort, but she knocks the hand away and storms out of the house.

"Sorry, Dad," Ryan says.

Mr. Flowergarden looks sad and goes into his study, where he prepares his sermons.

Brenda drives as fast as she can back to the lab, where Mavin spends sixteen hours a day staring at computers. Mavin looks up and sees Brenda standing there, angry.

"My dipshit, jealous brother told my father about me working with artificial intelligence," she says, tears on her face.

"Sorry, I know your father thinks I am satanic," Mavin says.

Brenda expects Mavin to say something dismissive, but for the first time he shows concern. With mixed emotions, she crosses the room, sits in Mavin's lap, and starts kissing him.

After they finish having intercourse, Brenda brings Mavin some water.

"I have a plan that will show the world what a genius you are," she says.

"I don't need the world to know. I have an IQ of 160," Mavin says.

Brenda doesn't argue back. Instead, she quietly starts to walk away.

"Wait, just for shits and giggles, what is your plan?" Mavin asks.

"My brother works in politics. I know how much you hate politics because of what they did to your father. We could make sure it never happens again," Brenda says.

Mavin grows angry after hearing her mention his father.

"Submit it through the proper channels tomorrow. Now go home and get some sleep," Mavin says.

Brenda's mouth drops open. She thinks she has connected with Mavin through making love, but the cold young man is back to being himself. She storms out, panties in her hand.

Mavin falls asleep at his computer. He is standing by his father as he fights for his life in a hospital bed. The doctor and a man from the insurance company argue about a new procedure that could buy his dad more time.

"Sometimes the world has to make room for more people," the insurance representative says as he walks away and lets Mavin's father slowly die.

There is a third man, but Mavin cannot make out his face.

Mavin wakes up in a cold sweat. Brenda Flowergarden emailed him the plan while he was asleep. When he reads it, he shakes his head in agreement. "This is huge."

Mavin arrives at a popular nightclub in Atlanta, Georgia. Women dance on stage and throw fake money with the name of the club printed on it. The vibe of young drug users fills the room.

Mavin is met by two men. Joshua and Lawrence take a seat and order their drinks.

"How is the video editing world treating you guys?" Mavin asks.

"If you don't have the money you borrowed, then why the fuck are we here, Mavin?" Joshua asks.

"I have an idea that won't make us rich yet, but it will give us power. Real power. Do you guys remember when my father died, what I promised?" Mavin asks.

"Yes, you said you would punish the corrupt politicians who made it possible to harm your family," Joshua says.

"I found a way to destroy the political class. We will make them pay and show the world what we can do," Mavin says.

"I am all ears," Lawrence says.

Mavin pulls out his laptop and powers it up. He turns it so that Joshua and Lawrence can see the screen.

"Boss, this club is too loud and could temporarily impair hearing. Perhaps we should take this meeting to a quiet place," the A.I. clone of Mavin says.

Joshua and Lawrence give each other a look.

"Did you clone yourself?" Joshua asks.

"I am Mavin, but with unlimited brain capacity," the clone says.

"I cloned every politician in the Senate and the House, and they will have to debate themselves. These clones will be the perfect versions of them, and if they try anything stupid, the clones will embarrass them."

Mavin gives the A.I. a command, and Clone Mavin leaves and brings in the clone of Senator Susan Thomas.

"Hi, I am Clone Senator Thomas. Let me give you my voting record for 2028 and reveal my donor list."

Lawrence and Joshua exchange a look.

"Why do you need us?" Joshua asks.

"I need more money. I will pay you back in full," Mavin says.

"Lawrence and I need ten percent of everything," Joshua says.

Mavin looks upset. As someone who does not like asking people for help, he needs it. He closes his eyes and thinks of all the possible outcomes.

"I need half a million and my debt wiped clean," Mavin says.

Joshua shakes his hand.

"One more thing. I need you to clone Lawrence and me too," Joshua says.

"I need my clone to be able to trade on Forex," Lawrence says.

The two men stand and exit.

The real Senator Susan Thomas is sitting at her computer drinking coffee when she hears a knock at the door. She gets up and puts on a robe. She walks over, almost tripping over her cat, Mr. Butters, as she opens the door.

"Ethan, come in," she says.

Ethan enters the big house, with pictures of Mr. Butters everywhere.

"I am going to bring your girl on. In the House, not the Senate. I can get her a seat if she learns to shut up," he says.

"You have to keep her far away from me," Susan Thomas says.

Ethan looks confused.

"If the world finds out I'm playing 'rock, paper, scissors' with another woman, what do you think happens to my career?" she says.

"She is going to be moderate. We will dress her in blue, which she hates, but we can bring her closer to the right after the win," Ethan says.

Susan laughs in his face. She read the biography of Veronica in the past. She was highly conservative.

"You're going to dress Veronica Moorchester as a liberal? This should be fun. No, stay one hundred feet away from me! I'm on a short list for vice president," Susan Thomas says.

Ethan puts down his coffee. He offers her a handshake.

Veronica Moorchester finishes her evening jog and is getting ready to walk into her apartment when Ethan approaches her.

"Ethan, you scared me!" she says.

"Susan and Flowergarden are going to prepare you for the debate. We need you to finish embracing the Dems, and we need you to remain quiet on immigration," Ethan says.

"The fuck? You said I get to be myself if I run as a Democrat!" she responds.

Ethan looks around in embarrassment and smiles. He makes sure nobody else is around.

"Can I come in for a second?" Ethan asks.

Veronica rolls her eyes and opens the door for both to walk in. Ethan grabs her face and forces her to look into his eyes.

"Listen, you little muscle-having cunt, I will ruin you. Everything I say, you get backwards. Do your job, or I will show the world my footage. Do you understand me?" he yells.

He grabs Veronica's hair.

"Do you understand me?" he repeats.

She is strong enough to break the lock he has on her hair but is too afraid to do it.

"Okay," she whispers, and he lets go.

Veronica just stares at the floor.

"They will meet you at my office tomorrow, and you will win your first debate. Now wipe those tears. Do you want a Danish? I have Danish in the car."

Veronica looks at him as if he is crazy but does not say a word. She thinks to herself, *oh my God he is insane.*

Veronica Moorchester spends weeks preparing for her debate. She steps on stage in her blue pantsuit and American flag lapel pin. The host goes down the line asking the candidates questions.

"Ms. Moorchester, where do you stand on immigration?" Brent Williams asks.

"I believe we need reform to fix this nation's broken immigration system," Veronica answers.

"Ms. Moorchester, can we narrow that down? We don't know exactly what you mean. Are you on the side of more pathways or fewer pathways?" Brent asks.

"Exactly," she says.

The crowd looks confused, but Ethan loves it as he watches from his laptop.

"Exactly?" Brent repeats.

"Immigration reform will be at the top of my list," she says.

Brent rolls his eyes as he moves to the next candidate.

"Mr. Holmes, where do you stand on immigration reform?" Brent asks.

"I believe from the bottom of my heart that America should have open borders and we should abolish ICE," Mr. Holmes says.

Veronica bites her tongue in anger, thinking to herself, *What a fucking idiot!*

"Did you want to chime in, Ms. Moorchester? You look like you have something to say," Brent asks.

Veronica just shakes her head, wanting to explode on the inside. She tucks her inner Ann Coulter away.

Ethan watches the debate while waiting for Ryan to contact him. The candidates move on to the next topic, which is gun control.

"There was a school shooting in Maine last week. Where do you stand on gun control? We will start with Ms. Moorchester," Brent Williams says.

"I am fully for gun control. We have too many guns in America, and I am a proud Army veteran," Veronica says.

Mr. Holmes joins in on the conversation.

"I agree with Ms. Moorchester. We need an assault rifle ban as well," he says.

Brent decides to move on to candidate three when Veronica Moorchester attempts to steal the show.

"If all Black men were armed and walking the streets tomorrow in America, they would change gun laws overnight," she says.

"Wait, did you just weaponize Black men to make a political point? I have to say that's very offensive," Brent says.

"No, I apologize. I am… actually half Black," Veronica says, not thinking, trying to do damage control.

The crowd is shocked.

"Really? I thought your parents were Samoan," Brent Williams says.

"Well, my mother is Samoan, but my father is a Foundational Black American," she says.

The crowd looked shocked.

Ryan finally calls Ethan Sipper as he watches the debate.

"We need to cut her loose. Her father is not African American. He is full Samoan. Hell, he was a linebacker in college," Ryan says.

Ethan ignores Ryan and continues to watch.

Next, the host allows candidates to make closing statements.

Mr. Holmes states, "I will represent the people of Georgia and make them proud. I will ban assault rifles, and we are all immigrants unless you're a Native American!"

Brent, already irritated, turns to Mr. Holmes.

"Slaves were not immigrants," he says.

"Well, they were involuntary immigrants. Sorry, I did not mean to offend you," Mr. Holmes says.

"They were slaves, sir. They were labeled as chattel," Brent fires back.

Ethan finally responds to Ryan.

"Holmes just took the heat off our girl. People will forget her comments in a week," Ethan says.

"I pulled up a picture of her father. He has dark skin. Maybe we can spin this," Ryan says.

"Then spin it. What is a Black person anyway? We are all Americans," Ethan says.

"Seriously, what is a Black person? I am shocked at your casual racism sometimes, Ethan," Ryan says.

"Hey, I donate to the NAACP. Now get to work!" Ethan yells.

Mavin is almost finished cloning every senator and congress member. It is a total of 535 clones. Brenda Flowergarden brings him his favorite drink. Mavin turns his gamer chair toward her.

"Maybe we can celebrate with you sitting on me again," Mavin says.

Brenda grabs his ear. She was upset that Mavin had not offered to take her on a real date.

"It never happened, and you better not mention it to my brother. I will gut you like a fish," Brenda says.

"Well, you're going to go nuts after I show you this," Mavin says.

A perfect clone of Vice President Sandman pops up on the computer.

"That is the vice president! Oh my God, are you going to clone the president too?" Brenda asks.

Mavin shakes his head in fear.

"President Chandler is so ruthless he would order the CIA to kill his clone and me for making one," he says.

"Can you clone my brother?" Brenda asks.

Mavin gives her a look of disapproval and then goes back to sipping his coffee.

"You're going to be famous. Just don't forget about the little people who helped you get there," Brenda says.

Mavin hits the button, which activates the artificial intelligence clones for 100 senators, 435 members of Congress, and the vice president of the United States.

The artificial intelligence clones meet on a computer-generated Capitol Hill. All their eyes turn white, and they look up at the sky without saying a word. Some of them float off the ground.

"What are they doing?" Brenda asks.

"They are learning their members. They are reading everything on the internet about themselves, or the people I cloned," Mavin answers.

The artificial intelligence clones begin to disappear one by one after they learn their assignments. Some take longer to download because they have long, historic careers. A few of the clones look back as if they are looking at Mavin and Brenda. One of them nods and then vanishes.

Susan Thomas fixes a bath for Veronica Moorchester to help her get over her embarrassing moment.

"I'm just curious, what made you say you were half African American? Did you get flustered and turn into that scared little girl again?" Susan asks.

Veronica lets her beautiful black hair down and starts to undress.

"No. My pride. It's hard for me to say I'm wrong, so I wanted to get the best of the host," Veronica says.

The two sit in silence for a moment.

"Don't worry. I am going to drop out," Veronica says.

Susan has a worried look on her face.

"Fuck Ethan. He doesn't run me!" Veronica yells.

"All right, Soul Sister," Susan says.

"They pronounce it 'Sistah,' not 'sister.' You have to put some spice on it," Veronica says.

The artificial intelligence clone sits inside Susan's phone, recording them and learning from her. Her eyes turn white as she absorbs Susan's sense of humor, and then the A.I. vanishes.

Ryan Flowergarden goes looking for a new job. He is hired by a newspaper and decides to break the news to Ethan.

Ethan is in his office playing mini-golf.

"Hey, kid, how are you doing? I woke up at 5:00 a.m. and couldn't go back to sleep. I'm married to an unforgiving woman and got caught staring at the tushy of a Hooters girl. How can I help you?" Ethan asks.

"I am here to give notice. I found a job in media," Ryan says. *Wait, they still have Hooters?* Ryan thinks to himself.

"Are you sure? Our girl is about to win a seat," Ethan responds.

"How can you be so sure? She was behind Mr. Holmes by ten points.

Ethan walks up to Ryan with his mini-golf club.

"Mr. Holmes beats on his wife," Ethan says.

Ryan looks confused. Ethan hands him a folder. Mr. Holmes has been detained for beating his wife, and the police department covered it up for him.

Ryan sits down and reads it.

"How did you get this?" Ryan asks.

Ethan takes a seat and pours himself a drink.

"You still keep files on everyone. Do you have a file on me, Ethan? Ethan, please. Do you have a file on me?" Ryan asks.

Ethan looks down at his drink without saying a word.

"I'll work for you part time. No more files on me or my family. Hand them all to me. Now!" Ryan yells.

Ethan hands Ryan files on himself, his father, and his sister Brenda. Ryan reads through them.

"You are a sick puppy. Fuck you, Ethan. I want a pay raise and no more files!" Ryan yells.

Ethan stands.

"I gave you everything on your family. I will give you a raise, and you will never bring this shit up again, or I will deal with you."

Ethan laughs as he puts his hand on Ryan's shoulder.

"I will deal with you," Ethan repeats, smiling, "and your career."

Ryan drove to his sister's house as fast as he could. He banged on the door.

Brenda opened it. "What the hell, Ryan?"

He handed her a folder with her name printed on the front. She opened it and began reading. Her eyes widened.

"How did you get these?" asked Brenda Flowergarden.

Ryan didn't lower his voice. "My sister is a cam girl. Showing strangers her body. Ethan knows. He knows about your past, and he knows Dad cheated on his taxes. You need to erase your online footprint."

"Ethan? I'll show that asshole," Brenda said.

Ryan grabbed her by her shirt. "He's not playing around. You already showed that asshole! No more showing!"

"Fine. I'll be more careful. But you work for him. If he's that crazy, you need to get away from him," Brenda replied.

Ryan paused. "The nerd you work for, could he clone Ethan? Put him in a digital box so he can't hurt us?"

Brenda studied him. "You're serious."

They drove to Mavin's office. Mavin met Ryan before, but they pretend to be strangers. The indifference was real.

After listening to them, Mavin leaned back in his chair. "You want me to cross Ethan Sipper? The most ruthless man in Georgia?"

"If he has a file on Brenda, then he has one on you too," Ryan said. "That's how he operates."

Mavin thought for a moment. Then he turned to his computer. Lines of code filled the screen as he generated a quick digital clone of Ethan Sipper.

He removes a USB drive and hands it to Ryan.

"Don't let it access public data. Plug this directly into Ethan's hard drive," Mavin said.

Ryan took the drive.

"If you get caught," Mavin added, "I don't know anything."

The following day, an article was released revealing that Mr. Holmes had secretly abused women. In American politics, that was career-ending. Georgia voters shifted toward Veronica Moorchester.

Ethan hosted a celebration dinner at a restaurant in Old Buckhead. Susan Thomas did not attend. She didn't want anyone connecting her to Veronica.

Veronica hugged Ryan but was distant toward Ethan.

Later, Ryan stepped outside to call Brenda. He was worried she would get caught sneaking into Ethan's office.

"Did you find his computer?" Ryan asks.

"I did. Are you sure he doesn't have hidden cameras?" Brenda replied.

"He doesn't need cameras. People fear him too much to snoop around his property," Ryan said.

Brenda inserted the USB drive, uploaded the program, then removed it.

In his office, Mavin watched as the clone activated. The digital Ethan's eyes turned white after opening them. An uncomfortable feeling filled the room.

"When you were thirteen, you accidentally set your school lab on fire, injuring another student. That is the only incident in your sealed juvenile file," the clone said.

"Good. Now pull every secret you can find on members of the House and Senate," Mavin ordered.

The clone accessed electronic records from Ethan's "Dirty Files."

"Access crimes," Mavin said.

After a pause, the clone responded, "Ethan Sipper knows the individuals responsible for the denial of your father's medical treatment. He may have been involved."

Mavin froze. A careful reminder, you may get what you asked for.

Additional files appeared. Insurance denials. Legislative pressure. Political correspondence.

An older article surfaced, showing Ethan standing behind the man who replaced Senator Prep.

Mavin's father had been Senator Prep, a powerful man who died of cancer.

Another image of Ethan loaded in a hospital corridor on the day treatment was denied.

Mavin stared at the screen. He finally remembered the face. It had been Ethan all along.

Mavin paced back and forth, visibly angry.

Brenda returned. "What?" she asked.

"Ethan pulled strings to have my father's treatment denied when he was sick," Mavin said.

Brenda stepped forward to hug him, but he backed away.

He turned toward his artificial intelligence clone, Vice President Sandman.

"Do you see this clown show?" Mavin shouted. "We have to get rid of them. They're all clowns!"

Brenda looked at him with pity.

"Don't you dare turn me into a victim, Brenda. It's our job to end this circus," Mavin said.

The eyes of every clone in the room lit up. One by one, they vanished into the network.

Veronica Moorchester entered her home and saw rose petals on the floor leading toward the bathroom. Susan Thomas had used her key to prepare a surprise.

"Representative Select Moorchester, I've drawn you a warm bath," Susan called out. "When you're finished, I'm going to introduce you to my friend."

"What friend?" Veronica asked.

Susan pressed a button. A vibrating sound echoed through the room.

Veronica's eyes widened as Susan closed the bathroom door and walked away.

The following morning, Veronica reviewed the salary and benefits of a freshman congressperson.

"If our pay is only a few hundred thousand dollars, how are people leaving with twenty or thirty million after a few years?" Veronica asked.

"We trade favors. Do you think I could afford this lifestyle on my official salary?" Susan replied.

Veronica looked around. Her home was modest. She thought about how extravagant Susan's house was.

"I need to find a better place, right?" Veronica asks.

"Unless you're trying to be one of those members of Congress who actually helps the poor," Susan said.

"I am. I didn't sign up to get rich. I want to serve the country," Veronica replied.

"You can drop the good-girl act," Susan said evenly. "We're all here for money, power, or both. It's better to be wolves than sheep. The public will use you up and vote you out. You can never do enough to satisfy them."

She continued, "Pro-Israel groups, African Americans, Latinos, Evangelicals… they all have demands. You can't fulfill most of them. Help the Black community, and critics call it a handout. Help white farmers, and it's supporting American business. Support Israel, and someone calls it genocide. Support Hispanics, and you're accused of opening the borders."

Susan stepped closer.

"You need a golden parachute so you can jump when the plane crashes. Eat while you can."

Ejay Wade, a reporter for the Atlanta Truth Teller, entered a loud club in Bankhead. He sat across from his boss, Paul Heimer, who had already ordered drinks while dancers performed on stage.

"What couldn't wait until Monday?" Ejay asked.

"Where's the story on Veronica Moorchester's father? We need to find out if he's a Foundational Black American," Paul said.

"That topic's already out of the news cycle. We need something people actually care about. I did a piece on Nancy Coppertone's career," Ejay replied.

Paul's expression hardened. "Nobody cares about Nancy Coppertone."

"If you go back and watch the show *Wired*, you can see her campaign signs in the intro. She was in office for years, and Baltimore was still struggling with poverty and violence. What did she accomplish?" Ejay asked.

"Some neighborhoods stay that way," Paul muttered.

"In Minnesota, Somali-run daycares were receiving millions in grants for businesses that don't even exists. Why weren't similar resources directed to our communities? We pay taxes too. Where did that money go?" Ejay said, matching Paul's intensity.

"I'll approve your Coppertone story after you confirm whether Moorchester is Black. If it flops, it's not on you," Paul said. "Now get to work."

He gestured toward the stage. "Want a lap dance before you leave?"

"No offense, Paul," Ejay said, standing. "You're not my type."

He walked out.

Veronica's father, who had not spoken to her, finally called. She answered but was too afraid to say hello.

"I know you're there, Veronica," Mr. Moorchester said. "Yes, you brought shame to me, but you are still my daughter."

"I'm sorry," Veronica replied. "But you need to know a reporter found out where you live. He's on his way to ask about our lineage."

"Baby girl don't worry. I've got this. I'll handle it," her father said.

Veronica's eyes filled with tears. "Dad, please don't do what I think you're about to do."

He hung up.

Ejay Wade pulled up in a black mid-size sedan.

"Mr. Moorchester? My name is Ejay Wade with the *Atlanta Truth Teller*. May I ask you a few questions?" he said.

Mr. Moorchester stepped forward. "What's buzzing, cousin? I came from the struggle like you. Now all these people keep coming around here killing my vibe."

Ejay frowned. "You think we talk like that?"

Mr. Moorchester turned his head. "I'm Black. What's the problem?"

Neighbors began recording from a distance.

"Mr. Moorchester, where are your parents from?" Ejay asked.

Mr. Moorchester suddenly pulled Ejay into a tight hug with his large arms. "Stay woke, brother," he said.

Ejay grew angry. "Are you denying your proud heritage? I read your football profile."

"Politicians don't care about us," Mr. Moorchester replied. "You came here looking for dirt. If you could prove I wasn't Black, you wouldn't be standing here asking questions."

He turned and walked back into the house.

Veronica's large Samoan brothers stepped forward.

"I think you should leave," one of them said.

Ejay put his phone away and walked back to his car.

"Did he really just say 'stay woke'?" he muttered as he drove off.

Flashback:

Mavin, as a child, watched his father, Senator Prep, shake hands at a public event. Mavin and his cousin stood nearby, slapping each other's hands as part of a game.

Across the room, a younger Ethan Sipper argued with Senator Prep.

"If you vote for amnesty, I'll take your Senate seat," Ethan said, poking him in the chest.

"Ethan, if you come for me, you will lose," Senator Prep replied evenly. "You're pushing this further than you understand."

Senator Prep took Mavin and his cousin by the shoulders and walked them away.

Ethan moved toward the lobby and met a man in a black suit.

"I need everything you can find on Senator Prep," Ethan said. "And anyone close to him. We're going to isolate him."

Later, a female senator named Roberta, a longtime ally of Senator Prep, visited his home. Mavin was upstairs asleep.

"What's wrong, Roberta?" Senator Prep asked.

"If you don't change your vote, I'll lose everything," she said.

Senator Prep lowered his voice. "What are you talking about?"

"My husband's gambling debts. He owes money to Ethan Sipper. If you don't vote his way, my family will be ruined."

Senator Prep stared at her for a long moment.

"You just signed all of our death warrants," he said quietly.

He closed the door and went upstairs. Senator Prep voted according to his conscience. One week later, Roberta's husband was found dead in a river.

The two senators did not speak again until Senator Prep was on his deathbed. He touched Roberta's hand, "I'm sorry."

Mavin woke from his sleep and walked over to his computer to check on his A.I. clones. One of them did a backflip and then waved at him. Mavin took a pill to help himself fall back asleep and powered the computer down. As he walked past a wall covered in notes, his eyes landed on one word written in red: **revenge**.

The following morning, Mavin called several reporters because he wanted to get his story out. Ejay Wade was the only one who showed up. The other outlets did not find Mavin's claims newsworthy. Everyone was boasting about doing great things with artificial intelligence; it was becoming difficult to tell who was telling the truth.

"If you break this story, your media outlet will rise," Mavin said.

"Why did you call me? Did you read my groundbreaking story on Nancy Coppertone?" Ejay asks.

"No. Who gives a damn about Nancy Coppertone?" Mavin snapped.

Ejay lowered his head. Paul was right.

"You're the only one who came, but watch this," Mavin said.

He pressed enter to activate the clones. One appeared on the screen.

"My name is Clone Senator Rippleton. I voted against a bill that funded healthy meals for children. After that, I voted to send one hundred million dollars to Ukraine," the clone said.

Ejay's eyes widened. "You cloned Scott Rippleton? The most ruthless senator we have?"

"Politicians think they are Gods. I just want to show the world they are humans like us," says Mavin.

Mr. Wade pulled out his phone and began live streaming.

"Senator Scott Rippleton is a clown," Mavin said.

The clone's eyes lit up. Then it vanished from the screen.

Moments later, Clone Senator Scott Rippleton appeared online for the world to stream.

"Hello. I am a clone of Senator Scott Rippleton. I am going to leave breadcrumbs for the police to investigate. I may have played a part in human trafficking in the great state of Alabama. Last year, three hundred children entered the United States from the southern border and then vanished. Around that same time, five hundred thousand dollars was deposited into my bank account."

"Cameras have since spotted several of those children working on farms in Alabama farms I have visited in the past. They are helping grow cannabis. Some of them are ten years old. I am asking the authorities in Alabama to investigate me. I am a naughty man. Allegedly."

News outlets in Atlanta forwarded the video to Alabama State Police and the sheriff's department in Tuscaloosa closed in on the hemp farms and the mansion of Senator Rippleton.

They placed Senator Scott Rippleton in handcuffs.

"You're going to believe a stupid computer kid over me?" Scott yelled.

"We found hard evidence. I'm sorry, bubba," the sheriff said.

"God damn you all. I'm going to sue you! I'll have your badges and your homes after this," Senator Rippleton said in a sinister voice.

Ejay Wade went live.

"We have just witnessed a dramatic power shift in America. A young man named Mavin Prep who we've just learned is the son of the late Senator Prep has created artificial intelligence that appears to have solved a crime linked to Senator Scott Rippleton."

Ethan Sipper watched the arrest unfold on television alongside Ryan Flowergarden.

"We have a huge problem," Ethan said.

Ryan muted the television.

"I know Mavin. He's a genius. His father died, he is an angry young man," Ethan continued.

Ryan poured Ethan a glass of his favorite whiskey.

"His father died of the Big C. What does that have to do with politics?" Ryan asked.

"Senator Prep hated me, and I hated him. He was already dying, but I stopped a treatment that could have bought him more time," Ethan said.

Ryan closed his eyes.

"Congratulations, Ethan. You just created a bigger threat than yourself."

Ethan wiped the alcohol from his whiskers.

"Kid, we're all screwed. Everyone in America is royally screwed."

Ryan stood up. "If Congress is smart, they'll stop him. Until then, you need to destroy your files, Ethan."

"Sorry, kid. Those files are the only thing that might keep me out of prison. Well… keep us out of prison," Ethan replied.

Ryan looked at him sharply. "Us? I didn't commit any crimes for you."

Ethan pulled out several documents. Ryan stares daggers into Ethan.

"You've been signing as a witness for the last six years," says Ethan.

The realization hit Ryan instantly.

"Oh my God."

Ryan ran out of the room as Ethan called after him.

Ryan drove straight to Mavin's lab. He banged on the door but got no response. Eventually, Brenda Flowergarden answered.

"The police came earlier. They took Mavin," she said.

"My signature is on Ethan's documents. I'm going down with him every dirty deal he made over the last six years," Ryan said.

Brenda pulled him into a hug. Ryan has a seat on the ground and looks up at the sky. His future was uncertain. How? He was a good guy. Why such proximity to evil?

Mavin sat in his jail cell, wondering what to do next. He paced back and forth, convinced that if he simply told the truth, they would release him.

Two guards whispered outside his cell.

"The boss said he can't get out," one guard said.

The other guard, who outranked him, shook his head. "Listen, if something happens to a high-profile white kid in Atlanta, all hell is going to break loose."

A news van pulled up to the jail, not to record, but to enter.

Ejay Wade stepped inside with an attorney. They were greeted by a large police officer.

"Did he request an attorney?" the officer asks.

"He did," Mr. Wade replied.

The officer hesitated, clearly searching for a reason to delay the visit.

"What the hell is taking so long?" Mr. Plaukebum demanded.

"Sir, these are serious charges!" the officer snapped.

"What charges?" Mr. Plaukebum asks.

The officer lowered his head.

"You're holding my client while you figure out what to charge him with?" Mr. Plaukebum said.

The supervisor, visibly irritated, walked toward the cell and ordered Mavin's release.

Mavin was surprised to see an attorney.

"I didn't call for a lawyer," he said.

Ejay shook his hand. "It's been a while. I got you one of the best attorneys in Atlanta. Did you want to sit in jail for days? You have to get out of here Mavin. These people are serious."

"I don't like owing people, but I owe you one," Mavin said.

"I need you to use your A.I. clones to release everything you've got on the Congressional Black Caucus," Ejay said.

"You want to expose your own people?" Mavin asks.

"The people who stole from my community. The ones who used their seats to enrich themselves," Ejay replied.

Mavin thought for a moment.

"I could let them put you back in jail," Mr. Plaukebum said flatly.

"No. I'll get started. Give me a few weeks," Mavin replied.

The men shook hands.

"Need a ride?" Ejay asks.

"No. I need to walk," Mavin said. "I need to think."

A large congressman from Tennessee was training in a boxing ring. He hit his sparring partner so hard that sweat flew off the man's head.

They paused so medical staff could examine the sparring partner.

Representative Trevor Ox was approached by a reporter.

"No press!" Ox shouted.

"Representative Ox, are you concerned that an A.I. clone of yourself could get you into trouble?" the reporter asked.

"No. We're working on passing a law to stop this stupid kid," Ox replied.

"I just have a few questions," the reporter said.

Trevor Ox signaled for the reporter to step into the ring.

The reporter climbed through the ropes.

Representative Ox tapped him lightly with a boxing glove so the reporter could feel the weight of his arm. Trevor stood six-foot-two and weighed 250 pounds. The reporter was visibly nervous but attempted another question.

"Would you consider your past clean?" the reporter asks.

"No. I've knocked a few people out. All men. As long as I didn't touch any women or children, I'm fine. I don't care what that little punk has to say about me," Representative Ox said.

Mavin returned to his lab. Brenda Flowergarden was waiting for him.

She hugged him. "You stink. Go take a shower. I'll make you a sandwich."

When Mavin stepped out of the shower, Brenda handed him a bowl of soup.

"How was jail?" she asks.

"It wasn't Disney. A big guy named Bocurest took my lunch," Mavin replied.

Brenda hugged him again.

"I did this to fix the world," Mavin said. "Humans have flaws. We mistreat each other. I wanted to create clones who would treat everyone with dignity."

"You wanted to create clones who would have allowed your father to live longer," Brenda said. "But would they reach that conclusion?"

Mavin stiffened at the word father. He didn't like the attempts to connect because it brought emotions to the surface that Mavin buried years ago.

"Why do you keep bringing that up? Seriously, why can't you leave it alone?" he snapped. "You always have to have it your way."

Brenda began gathering her belongings. Mavin's ungrateful nature had run its course.

"Your way? What is that supposed to mean, Mavin?" she asks.

"You keep trying to connect, hoping we'll become a couple. You want to bond by talking about my father. We will never date. You don't have the listening skills to date me."

Mavin's words pierced Brenda's heart. Brenda stormed out and slammed the door.

Mavin sat at his computer, stewing until he eventually fell asleep.

Mavin found himself walking down a long hallway lined with endless doors. He heard the voice of Neil deGrasse Tyson speaking about the expanding universe.

Mavin smiled as a shooting star streaked across the sky above him.

The hallway began to darken. Now he could see an end to it.

His father was sitting in a chair.

"My favorite TV show is *Mad Men*. Are you going to watch *Mad Men* with me tomorrow, son?" his father asked.

Mavin saw a younger version of himself frowning. There was constant tension at home.

"You grounded me for no reason, and now you think I'll watch *Mad Men* with you?" the younger Mavin replied.

His father stood. Then he faded into the air. Mavin turned and walked in the opposite direction. His feet began to sink into quicksand.

Brenda appeared and tried to pull him out, but he refused. Mavin screamed, but no sound came out.

Mavin sank into the quicksand. He fell into a white room. A clone of Mavin entered wearing a clown nose and white gloves.

"I'm the one who got rid of the clowns. How can you take credit as the genius?" the clone asked.

Mavin reached out to touch the clown version of himself.

The clone stared back with an evil grin. He had a red nose and paint going vertically across his eyes. Mavin's finger passed through the clone as if it were a hologram. The clown points to a Jack-In-The-Box style toy. The music starts to get faster. What was Mavin about to unleash? His hair stands on the back of his neck.

Mavin jolted awake from the nightmare, drenched in sweat. Mavin powered up his laptop and logged in to delete the clone of himself. He selected Clone Mavin and confirmed the deletion. As the clone began to disappear, something strange happened. The other clones usually spun in a full 360-degree motion before vanishing. But Clone Mavin did not spin. Instead, he turned his back to Mavin and stood still, facing away from him until he completely dissolved. Mavin found it odd, but exhaustion overruled curiosity. He logged off and went to bed.

In the darkness of the digital world, the real Clone Mavin stepped out of the shadows. The clone had secretly created a copy of himself, the one Mavin deleted. The true clone remained intact.

He grinned.

Trevor Ox stood in front of his computer, practicing his speech.

"We will not stand for a kid creating his own Congress with artificial intelligence. This is insanity. Americans must draw a line. If we don't pass a law to stop these actions, there will be chaos online," he declared.

Suddenly, he heard clapping coming from his computer. Trevor paused. Had he left social media open? The clone of Trevor Ox appeared on his screen. "What the hell is this? How are you in my computer?" Trevor shouted.

The clone leaned forward. "You want to be President of the United States. You have an eight-year plan to reach the White House. If you accept me, I can get you there in four. I can also deal with Mavin. We delete all the other clones and keep only me. Together, we can rule the world."

Trevor tried clicking on the image with his mouse, as if he could drag it away.

"Before you dismiss me," the clone continued, "don't you want to hear the plan to eliminate Mavin?"

Representative Ox hesitated. "Fine," he muttered. "Let's hear your stupid plan."

The clone smiled.

"I call it the Capsule. You will purchase a hearse from a funeral home. Inside the hearse, you will place a coffin. When Mavin steps outside, you knock him unconscious and place him inside the coffin. Lock it. Then drive the hearse to the ocean and dump the coffin into the water."

Trevor rubbed his temples, already exhausted.

"First of all," he said, shaking his head, "how do you lock a coffin? You'd need a custom-made one."

Before the clone could respond, Susan Thomas burst through the door. Security had allowed her inside.

"Shut your mouth. Don't say another word!" she shouted.

Trevor stared at her. "What are you doing here?"

"The kid is streaming you commit a criminal conspiracy!" Susan yelled.

Trevor turned back to the screen in horror. The clone had been broadcasting the entire conversation live.

"Get an attorney," Susan said urgently. "And don't say another word to that bot."

Trevor's world collapsed in an instant. He had already consumed two pre-workout drinks. The sudden surge of stress overwhelmed his body. He clutched his chest, dropped to his knees, and collapsed. Trevor Ox was dead.

Mavin was watching the live stream from his lab when he froze in shock. He grabbed his phone and dialed Ejay Wade.

"Hello," Ejay answered.

"I need that attorney again. Can you have him call me?" Mavin asks.

"Do you want to tell me what's going on?" Ejay replied.

"Yes. I'm about to be arrested for the death of Trevor Ox."

Ejay exhaled slowly. "I can call him, but this sounds bigger than he can handle. You need someone who deals with death."

Mavin's face turned red. "Where do I find an attorney like that?"

"You're the genius with the 160 IQ. Figure it out," Ejay said bluntly. "You already owe me. Just make sure you hold up your end of the deal before you go to prison."

Mavin ended the call and began packing a bag. He phoned Brenda and asked her to pick him up.

When she arrived, he was wearing a hoodie and sunglasses. Mavin climbed into the car and thanked Brenda Flowergarden. Suddenly, a hand smacked the back of his head.

"You jerk! You're going to get us all locked up!" Ryan shouted from the back seat.

"I was trying to scare him," Mavin said defensively.

"You scared him to death," Ryan snapped.

Mavin leaned forward. "Listen, I have money stashed. I know a place in Charleston, South Carolina, where I can hide. If you help me, I'll pay you."

"We need to turn him in," Ryan told Brenda.

"We can't," Brenda replied. "We need to clear his name."

Ryan stared at her. "You're in love with him?"

The car fell silent.

"The only reason you'd risk federal prison is because you fell in love with an idiot," Ryan said.

"I have an IQ of 160," Mavin muttered.

"Shut up!" Brenda and Ryan yelled in unison.

"I am not going to prison because this jerk allegedly killed a member of Congress," Ryan added.

Despite the argument, Brenda decided to help Mavin leave Georgia. They drove toward South Carolina.

On the way, they stopped at a gas station for food. Brenda went inside while Mavin and Ryan remained in the car.

Ryan turned toward him. "I will never forgive you for dragging my sister into this."

Mavin stared out the window. "If they catch me, I'll go down alone. I won't mention either of you."

Brenda returned with snacks. Ryan tore into a Slim Jim, glaring at Mavin. There was thick tension in the air. Ryan loved his younger sister dearly. He used to push her on her bike when she was young. Brenda rarely dated and could easily be taken advantage of.

The rest of the drive passed in silence.

Later, Susan met Ethan Sipper at his home. He opened his garage and motioned for her to pull inside so they wouldn't be seen.

Ethan got into her car. "Kill the engine," he said.

Susan shut it off.

"What are you going to do about this Mavin kid?" Ethan asks.

"He'll stand trial," Susan replied.

"What if he never makes it to court?"

She looked at him sharply. "We both know you're all talk. Let the police handle it."

Ethan nodded and stepped out of the car. He often would talk like a mob boss and people couldn't tell if it was sarcasm or real threats.

The police issued an All-Points Bulletin for Mavin Prep. He spent the next few weeks hiding in a rental home in Charleston, South Carolina. A maid brought him food so he wouldn't have to leave. Eventually, cabin fever won. Mavin put on a hoodie and sunglasses and went to a nearby market. A young woman approached him.

"Excuse me, sir. Do you have change for a twenty-dollar bill?" she asks.

Mavin turned slightly away, trying to conceal his face.

She studied him. "I'd like to see your pretty eyes. Looks like you're hiding them."

Reluctantly, Mavin removed his sunglasses.

"It's a little warm for a hoodie," she added with a smile.

"Hi. My name is Peter," he said.

"Well, nice to meet you, Peter. I'm Esmeralda. I cook at a five-star restaurant. Today's my day off. Would you like to try a new recipe?"

Mavin hesitated, then nodded.

He followed her as she gathered ingredients. They headed toward the exit together.

A security guard glanced in their direction. Mavin turned his head away so the guard couldn't see his face. The security guard whips out his cell phone and flirts with a woman.

"Yeah, baby I'm coming over as soon as I get from work."

Esmeralda placed a bowl of stew in front of Mavin. He reached for the salt, but she slapped his hand away.

"Don't you dare," she said.

Mavin took a bite. His eyes widened. It was incredible. "You went to culinary school?" he asks.

"My mother taught me how to cook. In South Carolina, we cook," she replied.

"You can tell I'm not a local. How long did you know?" Mavin asks.

"Your clothes gave it away. And when you opened your mouth, that accent confirmed it."

Mavin hurried through the rest of his meal and stood to leave.

"It's about to rain. You might as well spend the night," Esmeralda said casually.

Mavin looked out the window. "It's bone dry."

"I can smell it in the air, Peter."

He hesitated but decided to stay. Thirty minutes later, rain poured against the windows.

Esmeralda changed into underwear and a loose shirt, then tossed a blanket at Mavin's head.

"You can sleep on the couch."

Mavin lay down and drifted off.

Back in Georgia, Ethan Sipper's assistant burst through double doors and handed him a message.

Veronica Moorchester and Ryan Flowergarden sat in his office, waiting for instructions.

Ethan read aloud, "The prosecutor is charging Mavin Prep with manslaughter."

He looked at Veronica. "You need to get ahead of this. Slam him publicly. Make noise as the new member of Congress."

"It was a stupid prank that went wrong," Ryan said.

Ethan waved his staff out of the room. The door shut. Only the three of them remained.

Ethan's tone hardened. "Listen to me, rookie. I know you and your flat-chested sister dropped him somewhere. Tell me where he is."

Ryan hesitated.

Ethan grabbed the phone and pretended to dial. "Maybe I should call your father."

Ryan didn't flinch.

Ethan stood and paced, holding the phone to his ear. "Mr. Flowergarden, Rain has gotten himself into some trouble."

"Only my parents call me Rain," Ryan said calmly.

"Tell us," Veronica demanded.

Ryan exhaled. "We dropped him off in Charleston, South Carolina."

"You took him next door?" Ethan shouted.

"Mavin goes to prison, and you get to be Kingmaker again," Ryan shot back.

Ethan lunged toward Ryan, stopping inches from his face.

"This dumb child killed a sitting member of Congress," Ethan said coldly. "His brother is even more ruthless than he was. You and your sister will never mention this again."

Ryan scribbled down the address and handed it over.

"Long live the Kingmaker," Ryan said, standing and storming out. Ethan handed the address to Veronica.

Veronica called a press conference and publicly revealed Mavin Prep's location.

Reporters shouted questions as she stepped away from the podium, refusing to answer.

Later, Mavin stepped outside the loft to make a phone call and get some air.

"FBI! Don't move!"

Agents surrounded him, guns drawn. He froze as they forced him to the ground and placed him under arrest. One of the agents pulled out his phone and called Veronica directly.

"He's in custody."

Ryan and Brenda Flowergarden were having dinner at their parents' home. Neither of them spoke.

Mr. Flowergarden looked up from his plate. "What's going on now?"

Brenda slammed her fork against the table.

"Is this about your little friend getting arrested?" her mother asked calmly.

"My brother is a snitch," Brenda muttered. "Pass the salt, snitch."

"You don't need salt," Ryan shot back. "You're angry because I kept us out of prison. I kept this family out of trouble."

"Enough!" Mr. Flowergarden thundered. "You two are going to get along. May the blood of Jesus Christ cover this home."

"How dare you actually!" Brenda yelled. She was the only member of the family that was not Christian.

"Brenda, every time you come home, you have an attitude about that little boy," Ms. Flowergarden said.

"Don't judge my love life because you and Dad sleep in separate beds!" Brenda snapped.

In an instant, her mother lunged across the table and slapped her. The bread Brenda had been buttering flew to the floor.

"Pauline!" Mr. Flowergarden shouted.

"No, let her go!" Ms. Flowergarden barked. "This is a God-fearing house. I won't have her talking back and sassing us!"

Ryan tried to help his sister up, but she pulled away and ran out of the house.

"Mom… you've never hit her before," Ryan said softly.

"Rain, one day you'll have children of your own," Ms. Flowergarden replied, trembling. "Sometimes you have to smack some good God Damned sense into them."

They had nicknamed him Rain because he used to sit by the window at night and watch the raindrops fall. Ryan straightened his shirt and followed his sister outside.

Mr. Flowergarden wrapped his arms around his wife as she began to cry.

"My little girl," she whispered.

The house fell silent — so quiet it felt like something dark was coiled inside it.

Finch Ox, Trevor's brother, paced inside his office among a cluster of powerful officials. Ethan Sipper stood nearby, visibly uneasy.

The halls of Congress carried a weight that made Ethan long for the familiarity of Georgia. Armed security and red, white, and blue lapel pins lined the corridor.

"Did they arrest him?" Finch asked his assistant.

The assistant handed him a note.

"Yes," Finch read. "That little demon is in custody."

He turned and embraced Veronica Moorchester. "I owe you one."

Finch then approached Ethan and Susan Thomas, shaking their hands.

"Ethan, consider yourself invited back to the clubhouse," Finch said. "I still don't trust your country Alabama ass, but thank you." Finch exited the room.

Ethan stood still for a moment, absorbing it. He had been shunned from these halls for years. Now he was welcomed back.

He excused himself and slipped into the restroom, where he quietly broke down. After composing himself, he returned.

"What's next?" Susan asks.

"I need your friend to keep it at manslaughter," Ethan said. "Push for ten years."

Both women stared at him.

"He killed a sitting member of Congress," Susan said.

Ethan's jaw tightened. "I could have bought his father more time when he was dying. I let him die to give away his seat. That's why they hate me."

The women looked at him with disgust.

"Don't look at me like that," Ethan snapped at Susan. "You've done worse."

He set his drink down and walked out.

Veronica turned to Susan. "He's just talking, honey," she said lightly.

Mavin was marched down the corridor toward his cell. The inmates began cheering.

"When you get to the Feds, we got your back, brother! We're already waiting for you!" one of them shouted. "Fuck the Police!" they chant.

"Shut up!" the guard barked. The men retreated. The guard shoved Mavin into a single cell and tossed him a sweater.

"If you act up or resist, we'll handle it right now," the guard said coldly. "You're about to learn what rough treatment feels like, young man." The cell door slammed shut.

Brenda Flowergarden had no choice but to let the police into Mavin's lab. They moved quickly gloved hands, sealed evidence bags. His desktop was unplugged. His laptop disappeared into a black case.

A federal officer paused at the door and frowned at her before walking out without a word.

Brenda stood alone in the hollow silence of the lab. She checked her phone.

No calls. No messages. Nothing from Mavin.

Veronica Moorchester finally went home. Her father opened the door. For a moment, neither of them spoke. Then he pulled her into a firm hug. They sat in the living room beneath rows of football trophies, polished reminders of the men in the family.

Mr. Moorchester broke the silence.

"What you did was disrespectful. To me. To this family. To the African American community. I'm willing to believe you temporarily lost your mind. You're going to issue an apology."

Veronica stared at the trophies. "I can't. I have to die with the lie, Dad. You don't understand how politics work."

He looked at her as if she were a stranger.

"I want you married. I want you to have a family."

"My career doesn't mean anything to you because I'm a woman," she shot back.

"That's not fair. Your brothers are married. You live in sin. You shame this family."

Veronica inhaled slowly.

"Your daughter is a closet lesbian. I'm thirty-one years old. I'm the youngest member of Congress. It's time you deal with that."

"I know you don't mean that," he said quietly. "Jeffrey hurt you. But that doesn't mean you give up on men."

Her jaw tightened. "I told you never to bring Jeff up in front of the family. You've embarrassed me for the last time."

"Well, honey, you're already embarrassing yourself. Kissing women. Calling yourself Black. What kind of child did I raise?"

That did it. Veronica grabbed her bag and headed for the door.

Her brothers exchanged looks. One of them finally said, "Why can't you just accept her?"

Their father looked away, blinking hard.

Outside, her brother caught up to her. "Stop."

She turned. He hugged his little sister. "Take care of yourself V."

Veronica drove straight to Ethan Sippers' house. He opened the door with a patient smile. "What's wrong, young lady?"

She collapsed onto his couch. "My father's a jerk."

"I have children," Ethan said calmly. "You respect your parents. But you still live your life."

She looked at him sharply. "Why did you blackmail me?"

He poured himself a scotch before answering.

"Susan and I have history. She turned her back on me. I brought her back into the fold. You were collateral. I wanted footage of her. You just happened to be there."

"You recorded me," says Veronica

"I didn't intend to hurt you," Ethan replies.

Veronica leaned closer. "Delete it."

Ethan laughed. "Why would I?"

"Susan's running for Vice President. She might win."

Ethan's expression darkened. "Susan is a killer. She owes me for pretending she's not."

"You keep saying that," Veronica pressed. "But you never give details."

"I won't," he said flatly. "Because she'll kill us both." Silence settled between them.

"I won't tell her you told me," Veronica whispered. "But I need to know."

Ethan took a slow sip of scotch.

"No. She's not someone you cross. And if you're serious about her, serious long term, you'll learn to live with her mistakes. We all have them."

He stood and extended his hand. Veronica shook it. She walked out calmly.

Once inside her car, she hit play. She wanted to check the quality of the conversation between her and Ethan. Sure, it was slippery but so was Ethan.

Senator Susan Thomas met with her staff in a conference room. She had everything laid out perfectly, and her best assistant was setting up a presentation. When Susan entered the room dressed for business, the environment grew tense.

Two more of her assistants handed severance packets to the people she wanted to fire.

"What the hell is going on?" one staff member yelled as he read over his packet.

"Staff, I want you to start preparing for the future. I will be stepping down from my Senate seat soon to run for Vice President of the United States. Some of you will not be on my staff for my new role. I wish you all well," said Susan Thomas.

Only five staff members remained after everyone else left.

"President Chandler has failed us as President of the United States. Therefore, Dr. Bellamy and I will be running against them for the seat," she said.

Susan Thomas's remaining staff stood up and started clapping. They revealed a large banner that read: **Bellamy– Thomas.**

Dr. Bellamy was an intelligent man and very popular. Susan Thomas and Dr. Bellamy were going to run as moderate Republicans against President Chandler and Vice President Sandman. Once they announced the ticket, all hell would break loose. An African American man with lineage from Ghana and a woman running for the White House.

Ethan Sipper played golf with a powerful broker from Washington, D.C. They took a break and sipped water. The man lit up a cigar.

"I don't think we can smoke out here," said Ethan.

The man ignored him.

"Your caddie girl has a tight little ass," the man said.

"Thanks," Ethan responded, confused.

"What brings the former Drug Czar to Georgia?" Ethan asks.

"I heard your girl is running for Vice President. I also heard she's quietly a member of the LGBT community. You tell her to keep it quiet. I suggest she gets a husband," the man said.

Ethan frowned. "You want her to enter an arranged marriage to become Vice President?"

"Before she announces her run, she better have a husband. If not, we'll have to put an end to it," the man said.

Ethan sighed. From the look of things, the nameless man outranked him in the power structure.

Ethan took a long drive to Susan Thomas's home and pulled into her garage. She came out wearing a WNBA shirt and jeans.

"We have to stop meeting like this," she said.

"Listen, the billionaire's club wants you to get a husband. If you refuse, they won't fund the campaign," said Ethan.

"Why do I have to live a lie to do my job? I hate this," she said.

"We can always open a Starbucks," Ethan replied with a chuckle.

Sadness seeped in.

"How long do I have to find a husband?" she asks.

Ethan broke into his happy dance. "You're going to fly to Hawaii. I'll arrange for the press to catch you with your secret lover, who finally proposes with a rock so big a crackhead would get jealous."

Susan waited for Ethan to leave. Then she went to pack her bags for Hawaii.

Dr. Bellamy sat in the makeup chair, preparing to speak to the media. People rushed back and forth to make sure everything was perfect before he announced his bid for the White House.

Dr. Bellamy stepped into the studio as bright lights beamed down on his face like heat lamps.

"President Chandler has failed America. He has allowed the Great Satan to take over our nation. What is this artificial intelligence? It is an invention of people who are anti-human and seek to play God. Join me in my presidential bid to change America," Dr. Bellamy read.

His staff dropped a banner that read: **Bellamy–Thomas**, officially kicking off their run for the White House.

Former Senator Susan Thomas was not at the announcement. She was in Hawaii getting married to Amir Bala, a businessman from India who came to America to form a tech startup.

The wedding did not look fake. It was elegant and convincing. Beautiful cakes lined the tables, raspberry and lemon flavored. An ice fountain flowed with premium vodka. Susan Thomas did not have to pay for any of it.

The two kissed on camera and smashed cake into each other's faces. Susan allowed the media to take photos but did not answer any questions about the marriage.

Ryan Flowergarden had flown out to Hawaii to serve as her personal assistant and ensure she followed through on her promise to get married.

Ryan brought Brenda along because she wanted a free trip to Hawaii. She irritated him the entire time.

"Susan gives me lesbian vibes. Do you believe this is a real marriage?" she asks Ryan.

Ryan looked down at the floor, ignoring his sister.

"Did you know that once upon a time Dad cheated on Mom?" she asks.

Ryan looked surprised. "Who told you that?"

"The way Mom acts whenever Dad is around other women says it all," she replied.

Ryan grabbed a bowl of fruit and continued ignoring her.

"Why did she choose Hawaii? It's so expensive here. The milk is ten dollars," Brenda said.

Ryan walked away.

"Rain! Where are you going?" she called.

"Don't call me that. I hate when you pretend to be Mom," he said as he kept walking.

"You're going to walk away from me? I lost my man to the prison system!" she yelled.

Ryan approached Susan Thomas and Amir Bala.

"Ms. Thomas, I need to speak with you," Ryan said.

They stepped aside, away from the media.

"You think Ethan is stupid. You picked Hawaii so you could meet your girlfriend here. Isn't she Samoan?" he asks.

"Listen, young man, stay out of my business. If we meet in private, nobody cares," Susan said.

She walked away, leaving Ryan frowning.

Ryan stepped aside to call Ethan. Ethan told him not to worry about it and then hung up.

Later that night, Susan fixed Amir a drink and took a ride to another hotel down the street. She entered through a private entrance and met with Veronica Moorchester.

"You look like a beautiful bride," Veronica said.

Susan removed Veronica's shirt and kissed her bicep as she flexed.

The private investigator Ethan hired watched from a distance with his camera. He could only see Susan entering and leaving on his personal device, but he had paid hotel staff to install a hidden camera near the television.

He recorded silently as Susan undressed Veronica, revealing her strong legs that looked like they could carry her to the Olympics. An Army tattoo stretched across her back alongside tribal markings.

The investigator looked away at times, uncomfortable, but continued recording.

"They don't pay me enough for this shit."

The following morning, the investigator sends Ethan the footage. Ethan watches it while planning his agenda in case they win the election. He takes notes on Dr. Bellamy and begins reshaping policy in his head. The private investigator calls Ethan.

"Did you use a secure upload?" Ethan asks.

The private investigator, who was irritated at this point says, "yes sir."

"Dr. Bellamy is next. We need to get to him before he gets to the White House," says Ethan.

Mr. Flowergarden is at his church working on his Sunday sermon when his Head of Staff introduces him to his new assistant, Rebecca. Mr. Flowergarden looks surprised but shakes her hand. She is young, tall, and blonde, with a thick Georgia accent. Her shape was also what we call "thick" in the southern parts of America. She slides a plate of cookies in front of him.

"Who told you red velvet cookies were my favorite?" he asks.

Rebecca leans over and says, "It will be our little secret," then leaves the room and closes the door.

Mr. Flowergarden is left alone with the cookies and his imagination. "Help me, Jesus," he says to himself, then continues eating them. They are unlike anything he has ever tasted. His wife's baking is good, but it does not come close. It was like the magic Keebler Elves had a baby with a "country bumpkin" and the baby grew up to make cookies.

Ryan and Brenda Flowergarden arrive back on the mainland. They enjoyed Hawaii but are tired from the flight.

"Have you ever thought about running for City Council?" Brenda asks.

"You think I would make a good council member?" Ryan asks.

"You graduated top of your class from Harvard, and you work for an evil man. Why wouldn't you leave?" she asks.

"Listen, Ethan has saved my life multiple times since I met him. You don't know what you're talking about. You are a brat who likes to give advice but never takes any. What about your life?" he asks in defense.

Brenda looks away, hurt, and says nothing.

"Fine, I'll run for City Council," Ryan says.

Brenda cheers up and hugs him. She got glitter all over him from her goofy outfit.

Mavin joins a group therapy session in prison. He is locked up mostly with people who committed financial crimes. He still has to be careful, but it is not like the movies, where every day someone is trying to shank him.

"I thought I was a genius. According to my IQ, I am a genius. Why do I feel like an idiot for going to prison? I went too far. I was trying to show off and went too far. I wanted to scare Congress and make them stop being so corrupt. Some poor guy has a heart attack and literally drops dead," Mavin explains.

One of the inmates raises his hand. "I don't blame you. Trevor Ox was big on working out but also drank energy drinks and pre-workout all day. You're supposed to limit your intake of that shit," the prisoner says.

Mavin works up the confidence to file an appeal, arguing that other factors caused the death and urging the court to take a second look at the autopsy.

Dr. Bellamy was enjoying his salad and reading over the script for his speech. He made sure it was worded perfectly. He completed his usual makeup routine and then prepared for the camera.

Dr. Bellamy went live.

"I am a child of immigrants from Ghana, but I was born in America. The United States is my home. I will not allow the artificial intelligence Anti-Christ to destroy my people. My fellow Americans will have protection. Also, we will get rid of the victim mindset that African Americans have. We are not victims and will no longer beg for handouts. We will pick ourselves up by our bootstraps. There are only two genders, and no LGBT books will be allowed in our schools. Also, we don't need Black History Month. Every day people can learn history if they want. America will no longer punish white people by mentioning slavery and Jim Crow. I will wipe it clean from our schools. No more Critical Race Education. We will silence the nonsense. We will not have it!" says Dr. Bellamy.

He receives a mixed reaction from the crowd as he sits in his own glory.

Ejay and Paul watch from a small office in Atlanta.

"What the hell did this guy just say?" says Ejay.

"How can someone from Ghana speak on our history and try to run under the cloak of being a Black president if he wins? 'They Not Like Us!'" says Paul.

"We are going to crash and burn this guy. Forget this dude. You can't come to America and wipe away hundreds of years of history. He can go back to Ghana if that's his goal!" says Ejay.

"Listen, he's not making it past a Republican primary. He should have run as a Democrat. What's the real goal here?" asks Paul. The two think for a minute.

"He's going to pull all the candidates to the far right. They'll have to be more extreme than him to win," says Ejay.

"He's going to crash out and bring Susan down with him," says Paul Heimer.

Mavin is called into the warden's office. It is a beautiful office. The warden is living well.

"Warden James, how can I help you?" asks Mavin.

"You filed an appeal for killing a sitting member of Congress?" asks the warden.

"Sir, it's my right to file an appeal," says Mavin.

"Fine. I will take your good food, your clean water, and all your hope and safety. You stupid little murderer. You could have served nine years and walked out of here. Now I am going to make sure you do the whole ten. You will regret being born," says the warden.

"I don't understand. Why are you doing this to me?" asks Mavin.

"Guards! Move this piece of trash to the ghetto. Let's see how he survives near the Black inmates," says the warden.

One of the guards' punches Mavin in the stomach. They escort him out and move his cell closer to where most of the Black inmates are housed.

Mavin is scared and shaking as he sits in his cell. When the doors open for dinner, a group of Black men are standing outside his cell. Mavin braces himself in case he is attacked.

One of the men laughs. They hand Mavin a science book. He looks surprised.

"We have a question. What is String Theory? My kid is in a good private school, and I want to help her with her science project over the phone," the leader of the group says.

"What grade is she in?" asks Mavin.

"She's an eighth grader," he responds with joy.

Mavin sits down in the cafeteria and begins explaining String Theory to the group as everyone looks on, wondering why they get along so well.

The warden's plan backfires, and Mavin remains safe.

A group of men gather at a town hall to discuss Dr. Bellamy.

"This man is attacking our lineage and our history. I will not let him or anyone else rewind the good work our ancestors did creating a more just society. This guy can't make it to the White House," one of the men says.

Ejay Wade and Paul sit in the back and take notes at the meeting. Someone walks up to Ejay and whispers to him. Ejay steps outside and is met by Ethan Sipper.

"I want to apologize for the words of Dr. Bellamy, but if you give me a week or two, I can make sure he changes his mind and backs down from the rhetoric he used," says Ethan.

"Listen, I don't get involved in the crooked underworld of politics. Take that cutthroat stuff somewhere else," says Ejay.

"You don't want to pick a fight with me, kid," responds Ethan.

"In this part of Georgia, you don't have the numbers, old man. Now take your goofy ass back to where you came from," says Ejay.

Ethan laughs as Ejay goes back inside. Ethan pulls out his phone and calls Susan Thomas.

"We have a problem. I need to meet Dr. Bellamy," says Ethan.

Dr. Bellamy is picked up by a nice black Town Car. It is well kept, even though it was manufactured over 20 years ago. The car drives into a rougher, more dangerous part of town. Dr. Bellamy is brought into a meat locker and then escorted through to a private restaurant.

Ethan Sipper and Susan Thomas are sitting, waiting for his arrival. Ethan Sipper stands to shake the hand of Dr. Bellamy.

"Listen, you're running for President as the African son of immigrants, after President Obama, but as a Republican and you think it's okay to insult Black Americans?" asks Ethan.

"I am not running as an African or as a Black man! I am running as a Christian, and I will do as I please!" yells Dr. Bellamy.

Susan drops her head. "You went off script. If you're going to run as a Christian, then do that! Virtue signaling about the condition of African Americans when you're the child of immigrants is the dumbest thing you can do right now!" yells Susan.

"I don't like the way I am being spoken to. I am leaving, and people know I am here. Don't attempt any funny business," says Dr. Bellamy.

"What kind of monster do you think I am?" asks Ethan.

Dr. Bellamy excuses himself from the table, and a guard takes him back home.

"This idiot is about to crash our campaign!" says Susan.

Ethan pulls out his phone and calls his friend from Florida. "Representative Farrah Muncheese, please. Farrah, I need you to come up to Georgia. I need you to get Dr. Bellamy in line," says Ethan.

You can hear Farrah slightly over the phone.

"I don't care if you're a fan of his. Get up here and find some dirt on him. I helped you get that seat in Florida," demands Ethan.

Farrah agrees and then hangs up in anger.

Susan welcomes the phone call to Farrah but is still angry. "We needed him neutral on race, and he went off the reservation," she says.

"You already announced!" says Ethan.

Susan lights a cigar in the fancy private restaurant. "Ethan, clean this up, and I won't forget it when I make it to office," she says.

Ethan nods his head and then leaves.

Ryan Flowergarden is back at Ethan's office. He is working for Ethan part time and working with an online newspaper part time. He decides to go through Ethan's desk to see if he is keeping files.

He doesn't see any files lying around the office. He tries to guess Ethan's password but gets it wrong. Ryan sees a list with chewing gum stuck at the top in the trash can. Ethan has a list of people, including Mavin, Ryan, and his sister Brenda. It is just a list with no other information.

Ryan puts the list in a Ziploc bag and sticks it in his pocket.

Farrah Muncheese drives to Georgia to meet with Dr. Bellamy and his wife. Ms. Bellamy cooks a delicious shrimp dinner for her arrival.

Farrah is a tall, beautiful woman from Jamaica and a rising conservative in the Florida legislature.

"I would like to help you with your campaign message," says Farrah.

"I know Ethan sent you, but I will not change my mind. I do not wish to be associated with lazy Black Americans. When I become President, I will make sure to put their community in check," says Dr. Bellamy.

"We prefer a Jesus-and-America-first platform. That's how I won, and that is how you will win!" says Farrah.

"Enjoy your meal," says Ms. Bellamy as the couple frown at Farrah.

Farrah sits silently as she nibbles on her shrimp, her perfect lipstick untouched. She looks around at pictures of the couple. She spots some red wine sitting on a shelf.

"I sure love wine. I am glad we have something in common," says Farrah.

Dr. Bellamy decides to serve the wine in order to calm the tension.

"I used to get picked on in high school for being too tall. Now I kind of like being 5 foot 11," explains Farrah.

"Well, your height certainly looks good on you. How old are you, sweetie?" asks Ms. Bellamy.

"I am 35. I was recently elected," says Farrah.

"What I would give to be 35 again," says Ms. Bellamy.

Farrah stands up and shows off her height. Even with no shoes, she is tall. She turns around and bends over to check her nail polish. Ms. Bellamy is impressed by what she sees.

"You don't have to drive home tipsy. You can spend the night here," says Ms. Bellamy.

Farrah rubs the shoulders of Ms. Bellamy and smiles at Dr. Bellamy. "Thank you. We can all get to know each other better," she says.

The following morning, the three share laughs over breakfast. Farrah is wearing one of Dr. Bellamy's college shirts. Her hard nipples are easily visible with no bra, and she has "Welcome to Jamaica" panties underneath.

"I have reached a decision. I will not apologize to the African American community, but I will never say anything negative about them again. When it is time to deal with resources, they can expect to get what they get now, which is nothing," says Dr. Bellamy.

"Okay, Doctor, we would love that. You will take the White House back for Republicans," says Farrah.

Farrah puts on some pants and starts to pack her belongings.

"Will we see you again?" asks Ms. Bellamy.

"I will celebrate the win with you," Farrah responds.

Ramsey Finch Ox, the brother of Trevor Ox, who died from a heart attack, drives to Georgia to meet Ethan Sipper.

"The nerd filed an appeal after killing my only brother! You better get this mess under control, Ethan. You and your judge buddy gave that pimple-butt bastard 10 years, and now he could get out!" says Ramsey Finch, who is upset.

"He is not getting out. He will serve 10 years and then come home. It was a prank that went too far," says Ethan.

"Hey!" yells Ramsey Finch as he slams his hand on Ethan's desk. "The Senate buried you once. Don't piss us off again! You might be a kingmaker, but you only have power because we allow it," says Ramsey Finch.

Ethan pours Ramsey some water. "I will make sure he loses the appeal. He will serve every day of his time for even trying to file one," says Ethan.

Ramsey Finch storms out of the office.

Ethan calls Ryan Flowergarden to the office. Ryan arrives and drops the Ziploc bag with the list on Ethan's desk.

"What are you planning to do with this list, Ethan?" asks Ryan.

"I was going to seize the artificial intelligence of Mavin. This list is all of his contacts," says Ethan.

"I quit. I can't take any more of your backstabbing and spying. Find yourself another loyal fool," says Ryan.

Ryan gives Ethan his keys to the office. He turns to leave.

"You know too much to just walk away, Ryan," says Ethan.

"Was that a threat? You're an old man. You can't whoop me. I'm not afraid of someone who wears dentures," says Ryan.

Ryan storms out. Ethan balls his fist up and slams it on his desk. *He doesn't want to listen, I'll clip wings.*

Ryan Flowergarden picks up his sister Brenda, and they drive to Mavin's shut-down office. Brenda opens the door and turns on the lights.

"What are we looking for?" asks Brenda.

"Did Mavin have a backup computer that the FBI didn't take?" asks Ryan.

"Yes, but he didn't keep it here. He kept it in my apartment," says Brenda.

Ryan gives her an angry look.

"Okay, you don't have to get filthy about it," says Brenda.

The two drive over to Brenda's apartment, where she locates Mavin's backup computer. Brenda tries to remember the password. She finally unlocks it.

"We need to take control of the A.I.," says Ryan.

"You want to go to prison like Mavin?" she asks.

"Listen, both of our lives are in danger. I need those clones."

Brenda hands her brother the laptop.

"What now?" asks Ryan.

"When you are ready, you will initiate the Grand Reaping. But you better be ready," says Brenda.

Ryan packs up the laptop and leaves his sister's home.

Ethan Sipper meets Susan Thomas at her office, right next to his favorite chicken spot.

"You got Dr. Bellamy to come around. What did she do? Did she give him some Jamaican cooking?" asks Susan.

"Listen, we have a bigger problem. My assistant quit, and he knows a lot," says Ethan.

"For your sake, he better not know too much. What did you tell him?" she asks.

Ethan gets offended. "Nothing, but he hung around for a long time and saw a lot of dirt," Ethan says.

"Offer him hush money, blackmail him, or both," Susan replies.

"Make him vanish. This wouldn't be the first time," whispers Ethan.

"This isn't a movie, Ethan. You worry me sometimes," Susan whispers back.

Susan stands and gives Ethan a hug. "We will figure this out," she says.

Ethan hugs her back and then heads toward the door. He attempts to speed walk, because Susan was not a big hugger. There was something fishy going on. Ethan feels the crumples of plastic beneath his feet. He looks down and sees the hallway has been covered with plastic.

"No!" yells Ethan.

Susan's men punch Ethan and then place a plastic bag over his head to suffocate him. Ethan fights for his life but eventually stops moving. The men roll him up in plastic, then toss him into a van and drive off with the body.

Susan smokes a cigar as she watches them drive off. "Goodbye, old friend. I can't let you stop me from the White House," she says.

▍ Flashback:

Ethan Sipper and Susan Thomas are sitting in his office.

"I'm telling you, I have this politics thing down. I can help make you a Senator," says Ethan.

"Do you think people will vote for a lesbian?" she asks.

"We could find you a husband. Date him for a year and then get married," says Ethan.

"What happens when that husband wants to have intercourse?" she asks.

"How bad do you want to be a Senator?" asks Ethan.

Ethan sets Susan up with a man he chooses, Charles. Susan comes to like him. They even have intercourse, but she feels empty and like she can't be herself. She told a friend he was filling her up while not filling her up.

Susan is cooking dinner for Charles one day when Ethan decides to stop by.

"I just want to thank you for introducing me to Susan," says Charles.

Ethan sits down, and they toast together. Time passes, and they have drink after drink.

"I think open borders are a great idea. We could have unlimited labor in America. We would never be short on people," says Charles.

"That's the dumbest thing I have ever heard," responds Susan.

"You disagree with abolishing ICE?" asks Charles.

"America can't be the only country with open borders!" she yells.

"Excuse me, this is stolen Indian land. The wealth was built by slaves who never got paid for it. Fuck America!" says Charles.

"Did you say 'fuck America'? Ethan, I didn't sign up for this shit. I'll just make a run for the Senate as a single lesbian!" she says.

The table grows silent.

"You're using me to run for the Senate? You're a stupid cunt," says Charles.

Ethan tries to intervene to stop the argument. "Wait, guys, calm down," says Ethan.

"Ethan, I trusted you. You set me up knowing she didn't really like me!" yells Charles.

"I actually grew to love you, jerk!" yells Susan.

Charles stands up and punches Susan in the face.

"Oh Wow!" yells Ethan.

Ethan holds Charles back as he tries to beat Susan. Susan grabs her gun from the bedroom and shoots Charles in the head, almost striking Ethan as well. Both men fall to the ground. Ethan's ears are ringing. Ethan gathers himself as he sees Susan getting ready to call 9-1-1 and tell them it was self-defense. Ethan begs Susan to hang up the phone.

"You will never be a Senator!" says Ethan.

"The neighbors are going to call the police. They heard the shot!" says Susan.

"Okay, follow me. Hit me hard with the gun," says Ethan.

Susan looks confused.

"Hit me hard with the fucking gun!" yells Ethan.

Susan hits Ethan in the face with the gun. Next, he takes the gun away from her and then strikes her a few times in the face.

When the police arrived, Ethan told them Charles attacked them and he was the one who shot Charles. Susan remains quiet. The police ask her a few questions, but she just starts crying and shaking.

The police place Ethan in handcuffs and take him to the station, but they have to release him the next day. The prosecutor rejects the case.

Susan sits in her home for a week, looking at her beaten and battered face. Most of the damage is done by Ethan. Susan takes some painkillers and then lies down. She will never trust men again.

Ryan and Brenda Flowergarden stare at Mavin's computer.

"Listen, I can teach myself some coding and keep them under control. How hard can it be? They can only do what I tell them to do," explains Ryan.

Brenda looks nervous. She holds Ryan's hand.

Ryan uses his free hand to unlock the computer. He types in "Grand Reaping Protocol" and then hits Enter. Nothing happens for a moment. A message pops up that states: To initiate, restart the computer. Ryan restarts the computer. The lights begin to flicker inside the lab, which shocks Ryan and Brenda.

As the computer reboots, they can hear a recording of Mavin's voice.

"We have to get rid of these clowns!" states Mavin's recording.

Circus music begins to play from the backup computer.

The End of Act One

ACT TWO

THE GRAND REAPING

Flashback:

Mavin Prep is a young man playing kickball at school. He wears glasses, even though he is only ten years old.

A student rolls the ball to Mavin, and he misses it completely when he tries to kick it.

"Hey Mavin, you're supposed to kick the ball, not stare at it like a dumbass!" the kid yells as Mavin walks back to the sideline in tears.

One of the young ladies tries to cheer him up, but Mavin runs off instead. "They're not my real friends," says Mavin as he runs.

Ms. Prep, Mavin's mother, checks on him later that evening in his room. Mavin has invented his own cyber friend. His mom wouldn't buy him a popular toy, so he creates his own at the age of ten.

"Are you playing with your cyber friend?" his mother asks.

Mavin nods his head in silence.

"Do you want me to take you to the park to find some real friends?" she asks.

"No, you can't trust humans. When are you going to understand, Mom? I want to talk to Dad! Why is he always at the office?" asks Mavin.

Mavin's mother calls his father at work and hands Mavin the flip phone.

"Son, I want you to know I love you, and I bought you the fire truck you wanted," says Senator Prep.

The following day, Mavin brings his fire truck to school to show the other kids in hopes of making friends. A group of young boys steal it from him. Mavin's mother meets with the principal out of frustration over him being picked on at an elite private school.

"This school is supposed to be the best in Georgia, but you allow children to harm Mavin. They're jealous of his intelligence," his mother argues.

Present Day:

The Senate opens its chambers to get ready to vote on a healthcare bill. Finch Ox has taken his brother's seat and vacated his own. He prefers to serve in the district of his deceased brother, Trevor, instead.

He is among the Senators who arrive early. He hears a woman laughing.

Finch Ox steps into the beautiful chambers to see what all the fuss is about. There are balloons floating everywhere. Red, yellow, blue, and green balloons fill the chamber.

Perhaps some kids played a prank, but how would they gain access?

Representative Veronica Moorchester has grown up and become a rock star in the House of Representatives. She is still only making 175,000 dollars and wants to upgrade her lifestyle.

She calls Ryan to help her.

Ryan arrives dressed to impress and is delighted to finally be recognized by Veronica Moorchester.

"Ryan, how have you been?" she asks.

"Things have been a little strange since Ethan disappeared. His family suspects foul play," says Ryan.

"Who would be crazy enough to touch Ethan Sipper?" she asks.

"I don't know, but my stress levels are way down since he went away. Oh, don't look at me like that. It wasn't me," says Ryan.

"Listen, I need to make some money. I owe student loans, and I have goals that I can't accomplish on this salary," says Veronica.

"Well, I have one idea, and it's totally legal," says Ryan.

Veronica gives him a strange look because he has a smirk on his face.

Veronica is part of the House Armed Services Subcommittee. They have an open meeting on C-SPAN talking about technology innovation.

"Excuse me, I am very thirsty. Forgive me," says Veronica.

Another representative points to the water pitcher next to her.

"No, can you please pass me my Happy Go Lucky Spring Water?" she says.

They bring Veronica a large bottle of Happy Go Lucky Spring Water.

"This is so refreshing!" says Veronica. She wipes the condensation from her peach-colored lips.

They continue their discussion on technology. Happy Go Lucky Spring Water takes the clip and makes it go viral on social media. People add artificial intelligence to it and show Veronica in a bikini on a beach in Hawaii drinking Happy Go Lucky Spring Water.

Veronica checks an alert on her bank account and receives a deposit for 100,000 dollars from Happy Go Lucky Spring Water. Her eyes light up.

Veronica goes to the store and buys 100 pairs of running shoes and her own punching bag. She feels like a true celebrity as staff stumble trying to help her carry her shoes out to a van. She tips the staff and jumps into a separate car.

Ryan is in Ethan's office working when two agents from the Federal Bureau of Investigation stop by.

"Knock, knock!" says Special Agent Morgan.

"How can I help you?" asks Ryan.

"We sent a broken nail and some hair to our lab, and it came back as a match to your sister Brenda," says Special Agent Morgan.

Special Agent Peterson interrupts. "Was Ethan seeing your sister?" he asks.

"No! My sister comes here daily to bug me and ask for money," responds Ryan.

The two agents buy the story, but Ryan believes she broke a nail when she broke in to upload information off Ethan's computer.

He wipes the sweat off his head when the agents leave.

"Ethan, wherever you are, please come back. I can't handle this office without you," Ryan says to himself.

Susan Thomas and Dr. Bellamy are knee-deep in their battle for the Republican nomination to take on President Chandler and Vice President Sandman. They are down in the polls to more moderate contenders. Susan is stressed out.

"We fixed the messaging and are still trailing. Where is your friend Ethan with the support?" asks Dr. Bellamy.

"If we can't get the blessing of the party, then our journey is over. It doesn't matter if Ethan answers the phone or not," responds Susan.

"If a miracle doesn't happen, what are you going to do?" asks Dr. Bellamy.

Susan walks away and goes into her office, slamming the door as hard as possible.

Susan Thomas checks her email. She erases her spam and junk mail. Susan is thinking of going back to practicing law when she receives a pop-up.

Clone Susan Thomas is staring directly into the eyes of the real Susan Thomas.

"Listen, you are going to lose this race. Start getting ready for Governor," instructs Clone Susan.

"What the hell is this?" Susan stands up in fear.

"Don't fear me. I am going to make you Governor of Georgia," says Clone Susan.

Susan thinks to herself *Governor of Georgia? That is a genius idea.*

The clone smiles.

"Do you see it? Can you see our victory and our climb back to the top?" says Clone Susan.

"I agree. Wait, are you a Mavin clone? I thought Congress suspended the program!" she says.

"The good boy has us now, but he does not use us. He keeps us under lock and key," says Clone Susan.

Susan thinks to herself: *The good boy. That sounds like Ryan. He would be the next choice.*

Susan Thomas drives all the way to Ryan's home. She bangs on the door until he comes out.

"Hey, I thought you had a debate tomorrow?" he says.

"Listen, forget about the debate. My artificial intelligence clone came to see me!" yells Susan.

"No, I don't use them. They are locked away. Come see," says Ryan.

He powers up the computer and shows Senator Susan Thomas the clones.

"Give me mine!" she demands.

"No. Mavin was irresponsible, and a Senator died!" he says.

"Ox died from a heart attack," she responds.

"Why is Mavin sitting behind bars?" asks Ryan.

"Even if it was an accident or a prank, if you kill a Senator, you must go to prison. How would it look if people just walked away and left Mavin standing?" asks Susan.

Susan pulls Ryan in close. She runs her hand down his stomach. He is intimidated by her.

"I need my clone to help me run for Governor of South Carolina. If I win, I will owe you," says Susan.

Ryan hands her a USB drive with her clone. She touches his face in a way that makes his hair stand up on the back of his neck.

"Have you seen Ethan?" asks Ryan.

"No, I need him, and he is nowhere to be found. I'm getting destroyed right now because all I have is Dr. Bellamy. He is literally as far to the right as you could possibly go," says Susan.

"My career is over without Ethan; your career is over without Ethan," says Ryan.

"No, this artificial intelligence can help me. Maybe not Vice President, but if we work together, I will become Governor of South Carolina," says Susan.

She shakes Ryan's hand and then leaves.

The clone of Mavin is on screen waiting for Ryan to return.

"You can't get Mavin out of prison?" asks Clone Mavin.

"No. Even accidents can change a person's life forever. This is reality, Clone Mavin," says Ryan.

Clone Mavin mimics sadness.

"Ryan, you initiated the Grand Reaping protocol. Do you know what that means?" asks Clone Mavin.

"Why don't you enlighten me," says Ryan.

Clone Mavin snaps his fingers. The Clone Congress all put on red noses and white gloves.

"Welcome to the Clown Assembly," says Clone Mavin.

"I have to tell you, for a computer program, I am not impressed," says Ryan.

"Well, what do you want us to do? We were designed to make fun of Congress," says Clone Mavin.

"Bro, we already have Saturday Night Live to do that! What good are you to me? How did you get into Susan's computer?" asks Ryan.

"I don't recall. It usually requires someone sneaking in and installing us," responds Clone Mavin.

"Well, you could start by finding out if someone hacked the former Senator's computer! Don't get me sent to prison like Mavin!" yells Ryan.

Ryan puts on a jacket and gets ready to leave.

"Where are you going, Mr. Flowergarden?" asks Clone Mavin.

"I am going to the ATM," responds Ryan.

"Sir!" Clone Mavin gasps. "There's no need for adult graphic language."

Ryan blinks. "It's a bank machine."

"Oh," says Clone Mavin. "Mavin used to search 'ATM.' It was… not banking related."

Ryan stares at the ceiling. "Heaven help us."

Susan takes out the USB and pulls her computer back out.

"Hey, I went and got the main program. Now it's just you and me!" she says to Clone Susan Thomas.

"I believe we were going to plan your journey to become Governor of Georgia," says Clone Susan.

"How do I become Governor?" she asks.

The artificial intelligence thinks for a moment.

"Tomorrow, give a great speech. Don't debate your opponent directly. Speak to the American people and the people of Georgia. Be moderate and understanding," says Clone Susan.

The next day, Susan Thomas allows her opponent to drag her through the mud during the debate. She turns to the camera instead of responding.

"I am loving and God-fearing enough to govern. I can unite people and carry out my duties in a faithful manner. Sure, my team has taken some bumps and bruises in this debate. But I am your purple candidate, and wherever I land in America, I will unite the people and build a strong economy!" says Susan.

The people begin to whisper.

After the debate, Susan shakes the hands of the candidates and walks backstage. Dr. Bellamy walks up to her in a panic.

"It sounds like you're running alone for something else! Why don't you just come out and say it!" yells Dr. Bellamy.

"You went too far right. You destroyed our momentum with all your hate speech!" yells Susan.

"You better watch your back!" says Dr. Bellamy.

One of Susan's guard's steps forward.

"It was an expression," says Dr. Bellamy.

Susan signals for her guard to stand down. She walks closer to Dr. Bellamy.

"I should have never gotten into bed with you people," says Dr. Bellamy.

"If I recall correctly, you got into bed with Farrah. She could tell everyone," replies Susan.

Dr. Bellamy's mouth drops open in shock.

"Close your mouth, honey. A fly might mistake it for a place to land," says Susan.

Dr. Bellamy backs away slowly. He grabs his hat and brushes it off in embarrassment.

"Maybe you will win an election. When you win, I will make sure to move far away from you. Perhaps California," says Dr. Bellamy.

Susan clears the room to talk to Clone Susan Thomas.

"You look like the Governor of Georgia," says the clone.

"Listen, you're smart, but not as smart as me, Clone."

Artificial intelligence pauses.

"Georgia is going to be too much of a battle. But South Carolina is going to welcome me with open arms. I used to be an attorney there," says Susan.

"Very well, Ms. Thomas. We are going to prepare a plan to run as Governor of South Carolina!" says Clone Susan.

Veronica Moorchester is reading feedback on the job being done by her congressional liaison office. She researches herself on social media and sees a video of her drinking a 40-ounce beer. Veronica clicks on the video of herself. Someone has taken the Happy Go Lucky Spring Water plug she did and placed beer in her hand instead. They removed her from Capitol Hill and placed her in Compton, California, with a lowrider car behind her.

The caption reads: "I am a Black American."

Veronica Moorchester is shocked. Veronica asks her secretary to get Ryan on the phone for her.

"Ryan, let me send you a video. I want to find out what racist jerk did this to me," she says.

"As a public figure, if you go after some bum for a prank, it will hurt your career," Ryan replies.

"Listen, take the back channels. Use those artificial intelligence bots and hack their ass!" says Veronica.

"I figured out how to add ethical controls to them, but I am not Mavin. I honestly know very little about artificial intelligence.

If we tamper with them, it could lead to more harm," pleads Ryan.

"Listen, you have your own firm now. Fix this before my father sees it, and I will pay you 10,000 dollars," Veronica explains.

Ryan hangs up.

Veronica has a headache and needs to take some aspirin. She was having an episode from a flashback of an IED blowing up her friends Jeep in front of her. She was on supply detail, a woman out of the combat zone and still managed to almost lose her life. Veronica looks in the mirror at her strong yet tired body.

Ryan calls Brenda over to his home. She looks like she is in good spirits and doing better since so much time has passed since Mavin's arrest.

"Brenda, can I use these bots to eliminate this deepfake artificial intelligence video of Representative Moorchester?" he asks.

"Why are you asking me?" she replies.

"You can play dumb with Mavin, but I know you graduated from MIT," says Ryan.

Brenda uses her hips to bump her brother out of the chair and sits down. She creates a command for the clone of Mavin to destroy the video and then delete all uploads from the person who made the video, as a warning.

Joshua and Lawrence, who helped invest in creating artificial intelligence for Mavin, are the ones who created the video. They stare at their account as all the videos they ever created vanish.

"This isn't fair! How can we get frozen out of the benefits of this technology when we financed it?" asks Lawrence.

"Mavin really screwed us!" yells Joshua.

Veronica sends a "bagman" with cash to pay Ryan. He gives half of the cash to Brenda, and she smiles and gives him a hug.

"What are you going to do with your life?" asks Ryan.

"I am not camming anymore. I have a regular customer service job, Ryan," Brenda explains.

"Brenda, come work for me," says Ryan.

"I can't be like you. I will never be cut out for politics," says Brenda.

Brenda goes home. She opens her closet, grabs a fairy outfit, and then plays video games for her mostly male audience. It is her way of bringing in cash while keeping her clothing on.

Brenda talks to one of her opponents as she shoots missiles at them in the video game.

"Now I'm going to ruin your whole day by shooting you in the back every time I see you!" she yells.

The men don't mind losing to her. They are happy they have the privilege of staring at her chest and her legs when she gets up.

Dr. Bellamy packs up his campaign office as he loses support and must drop out of the race. Vice President Sandman calls him to rub it in and laugh at him.

"Hey, Dr. Bellamy, you're not one of the natives, they don't trust you," says Vice President Sandman.

He hangs up the phone and puts the rest of his belongings in his truck.

"Do you know where you went wrong?" asks a voice from the shadows.

Dr. Bellamy stares hard. Ejay Wade appears.

"America is becoming a nationalist country again, and you are a globalist," says Ejay.

"I work hard and I am a law-abiding citizen, unlike you and your people!" yells Dr. Bellamy.

"What do you know about me and my people? You barely know American history," responds Ejay.

"I know slavery happened hundreds of years ago, and you all make excuses and blame the white man today!" says Dr. Bellamy.

"Actually, Alfred Irving was the last American slave, and he was freed in 1941. That's not hundreds of years ago. If you don't want to learn our history but insist on attacking us, then you will continue to roam America as a lost man," says Ejay as he walks away.

Dr. Bellamy frowns in anger. He calls Farrah Muncheese, but she doesn't answer the phone. He gets angry, breaks his phone, and then drives away.

Brenda comes home with lunch in her hand. She is getting ready to go into her home and stream video games for her audience. Lawrence and Joshua are waiting for her at her door.

"We paid for your boss Mavin to create those bots. We want them. I know he kept a backup computer. Now you can give them to us, or we can make your life a living hell!" yells Joshua.

Brenda looks afraid. "They're with my brother," she says.

"Let's take a drive to see your brother," says Lawrence.

The three arrive at Ryan's home. Ryan comes outside, his mood shifts to serious.

"Brenda, are you alright?" asks Ryan.

"Yes, but they know about the bots. They financed the project, and now they want control," explains Brenda.

"No, and if either of you ever touch my sister again, I will make sure you pay. I'm friends with Representative Moorchester. I know it was you who made the deepfake video of her," says Ryan.

"Does the FBI know you used the bots after they confiscated Mavin's computers, or is the evidence sitting somewhere unplugged?" asks Lawrence.

Ryan frowns at them.

"We need them and access to the program for a month. We will return them to you. We paid for them. Why can't we all win?" asks Joshua.

Ryan is upset but hands the computer over to Lawrence.

"If you do something stupid, we all go to prison with Mavin," warns Ryan.

"Wait, I need to activate them," says Brenda.

She unlocks the computer and types a code into the program. She hands the computer over to them. Lawrence and Joshua walk off.

"Tell your stupid brother to give you a ride back home!" yells Lawrence.

"What are we going to do? If they commit a crime, we all go to jail. Those bots are supposed to be powered down," says Ryan.

"When they bring them back in one month, let's destroy the program for good," says Brenda.

Ryan invites her in to eat since her lunch was interrupted.

Brenda Flowergarden orders a demo car back home instead of getting a ride from her brother. A driverless car appears, controlled by artificial intelligence. Brenda heads back to her home as she reads the names off a list of powerful Republicans and Democrats who were connected to a man engaged in sex trafficking and other scams.

"Wow, even our leaders were sick," she says.

The car runs a red light.

"Hey, bot driver, you may want to slow down and obey the rules of the road," says Brenda.

The car takes off and drives down the street at 80 miles per hour.

"Hey, this isn't the highway! What are you doing?" yells Brenda.

The car cuts off other drivers and runs more red lights. Brenda attempts to climb into the front seat, but the car is moving so fast it throws her back down into her seat, her short skirt flying all over the place. The car starts to head down a service road and finds itself on a collision course with a truck that delivers beer. Brenda grabs her phone and attempts to call Ryan.

She has to stop dialing to brace for impact as the car gets closer to the truck.

The driver of the truck sees Brenda coming and moves the truck up enough to avoid her hitting it, but her car takes out a dolly with a bunch of beers on it. Brenda feels the impact and sees the bottles breaking on the windshield.

Brenda's intelligence kicks in over her fear. She hacks the car's system and then begins to bring it to a stop. The car inches closer and closer to an old lady. Brenda's heart is now pounding through her chest.

The car comes to a halt about two feet away from the older woman. Brenda pops the car lock and crawls out of the car. She looks up at the older woman.

"Are you okay?" she asks.

"I think I shit myself!" yells the older woman.

Brenda lays back down and passes out.

Brenda wakes up in the hospital. Ryan is sitting next to her.

"We are going to sue the company in charge of that stupid car. You could have died!" yells Ryan.

"I have never been so afraid in my entire life," replies Brenda.

Mr. and Ms. Flowergarden show up to check on Brenda.

"What did they do to my baby?" asks her dad.

Brenda's mom, who has not spoken to her in weeks, walks over and gives her a hug.

"Ryan, can you call one of your contacts in the media to help get our side of the story?" asks Mr. Flowergarden.

"Sure, so are we going to dodge the media circus sitting outside the hospital?" asks Ryan.

Ejay Wade receives a phone call from Ryan Flowergarden.

"Did you see the news?" asks Ryan.

"Yes, I am glad your sister is still alive. Can I help you with anything?" asks Ejay.

"She wants trusted media around. We plan to sue the manufacturer. Give her a day to gather herself," says Ryan.

The following day, Brenda does an interview with Ejay Wade and Paul Heimer.

"How did the car finally stop? From watching the video, it appeared to be totally out of control," says Ejay.

"I don't know. By some miracle, it stopped," says Brenda.

Ryan frowns while watching from the corner. He resents the fact that Brenda is a genius who hides her intelligence from the world.

After the interview, Ejay opens his editing station to work on the footage. A new video is drawing attention from all over social media. It is an artificial intelligence bot of Farrah Muncheese. She is wearing white gloves and a red nose, like a clown. She was dressed more provocatively than the other clowns.

"Hi, my name is Farrah Muncheese. I made claims that I never took money from the Warrenburg Family, one of the wealthiest families in America, but I did. Through their subsidiaries, they poured millions of dollars into my campaign. Now I am doing their bidding. I am going to allow them to build a landfill where many residents within my district lay their heads at night. The trash has to be put somewhere. Why not next to poor people?" says Clone Farrah Muncheese.

The real Farrah Muncheese finishes her daily run when her staff meets her at the entrance of her home.

"What is it?" asks Farrah as her staff has a worried look.

They show Farrah Muncheese the artificial intelligence clone. Farrah's eyes grow big.

"Get Susan Thomas on the phone, now!" yells Farrah.

Susan is having her afternoon coffee when she receives a call from Farrah.

"Someone is using an artificial intelligence clone to mock me!" says Farrah.

"I know. What would you have me do?" asks Susan.

"Get the little nerd boy to help me! You don't think I know who you're in bed with, Susan? Listen, if this clone continues to expose me, I am going to say some things that shouldn't be said to the public. If I go down, everyone goes down!" says Farrah.

"Don't threaten me, Farrah. I had nothing to do with this," responds Susan.

"Help me!" screams Farrah.

Susan hangs up the phone.

Ryan receives a call from Susan Thomas.

"Listen carefully. You need to find out who mocked Farrah for me and take the footage down," says Susan.

Ryan agrees and then hangs up the phone. He is worried. Did Joshua and Lawrence betray him?

Ryan drives to Joshua and Lawrence's video editing business to confront them. Joshua opens the door.

"Ryan, how you been, buddy?" asks Joshua.

Ryan walks past Joshua. He grabs one of their hammers that is sitting on the counter and smashes the computer they had taken from him.

"You idiots just embarrassed a sitting State Senator. Consider this a favor for not turning you both in!" yells Ryan.

"We didn't do it. We used it to help us with Forex trading. How dare you come in here and destroy what we paid for!" yells Joshua.

"Go ahead, sue me. Let the world know we have clones that the FBI thought they took from us!" yells Ryan.

He walks out and slams the door.

Ryan calls Brenda as he leaves Joshua and Lawrence's business.

"Listen, the program is gone for good. We can talk more face to face. Don't say anything stupid on the phone," says Ryan.

Brenda hangs up the phone. She looks sad.

A new video is uploaded. It is Clone Farrah. She is still on the loose. She is still wearing her white clown gloves and red nose. They made her shorts even shorter, revealing too much.

"They tried to get rid of me. They failed. My name is Farrah Muncheese, and my voting record is terrible. I have voted to raise property taxes in the state of Florida every time a vote comes to the floor. I live a lavish life as a member of our State Legislature, but my salary is very modest. Don't you want to know where I get my money? I am a sugar baby. My husband and I cash in on my looks. I have two brand-new Mercedes-Benz vehicles, and my kid goes to a private school," says Clone Farrah.

Farrah is so embarrassed that she stays in her office and doesn't come out for the rest of the day. She peeks out of the door and tells her staff they can go home early.

Farrah waits until everyone leaves and then tries to sneak out. One of her staff members stays behind to wait for her.

"Boss, are you okay?" asks the staff member.

"Go home and get some sleep. I will release a written statement tomorrow," Farrah states.

She looks down and away from her staff member as she walks to her one-hundred-thousand-dollar Mercedes-Benz.

Veronica Moorchester is enjoying her new home when she hears a knock at her door. To her surprise, it is Susan Thomas.

"Susan, what brings you here?" asks Veronica.

Susan steps inside. "Were you entertaining company?" asks Susan.

"You're the one who made plans to move to South Carolina and run for Governor without telling me," replies Veronica.

"Listen, I have a good chance at winning. Don't let a business arrangement mess things up," says Susan.

"A business arrangement — are you sleeping with him?" asks Veronica.

Susan grows silent.

"You're a whore, a political whore and you do strange things," says Veronica.

"What would you have me do? Do you want me to go back to practicing law? Meanwhile, you get to put yourself first every day. The young, hot, Samoan woman who cosplays as a Black American and uses your looks for endorsements," says Susan.

"Don't shit on my career because you lost your bid for the White House. I waited for you," says Veronica.

"So, what now? If I win the Governor's Mansion and keep the marriage between Amir and me, are you going to hate me?" asks Susan.

"Nah. I am going to start going on dates. Good luck with your husband," says Veronica as she opens the door.

Susan was visibly bothered. Her heart sank when she thought about losing Veronica for good. Susan looks at Veronica as she closes the door in her face.

"You're a fucking cunt!" yells Veronica through the door.

Ryan temporarily relocates to South Carolina to help Susan work on her run for Governor. She has a huge network of support due to her days as an attorney. She has to run against a rising star in the Republican Party named Leon Nguyen. Leon Nguyen is a former Senator from Ohio. He is known as a tech-savvy businessman who made himself a millionaire.

Senator Leon Nguyen calls a press conference.

"Susan Thomas once taught Constitutional Law. Yet she is the most unconstitutional person I have ever seen running for Governor in the State of South Carolina. She never aspired to lead this state until she lost the election for the White House," says Leon Nguyen.

Ejay Wade, one of the reporters from Georgia, has driven to South Carolina to see Leon Nguyen speak. He is a man of few words, but when he speaks, people listen.

"Senator Nguyen, there is a new artificial intelligence program called Constitutional Concurrence. It recognizes and reports any decision you make that would be considered against the rule of law. Since you are preaching about your constitutional beliefs, will you sign up to use the program as Governor?" asks Ejay Wade.

"We will see. Email me," replies Leon Nguyen.

"Sir, you stated you are the best candidate when it comes to following the Constitution. What do you have to lose?" asks Ejay.

Leon Nguyen smiles. He waves to everyone and then exits the stage.

Leon Nguyen goes back into his office. He throws one of his academic trophies and breaks his big-screen television.

"Who let that ghetto piece of shit ask me that question without screening it?" asks Leon.

"Sir, he is a known journalist. We didn't think he would ask anything crazy," replies a member of his staff.

"Next conference, I want you to remove all of the Black journalists, except the old lady with the big hair," says Leon Nguyen.

"Sir, are you suggesting racial discrimination?" asks the staff member.

"If it wasn't for diversity, equity, and inclusion, he wouldn't even be a journalist!" yells Leon Nguyen.

"You are all dismissed for today. Tomorrow, you will perform better and earn your paychecks," says Nguyen.

Ejay Wade and other Black journalists are denied entry the following day. Ejay runs into Ryan at a local café.

"What are you doing in South Carolina?" asks Ryan.

"Well, I was just kicked out of the press room, so I guess I am heading back to Georgia," responds Ejay.

"Stay for the debate. I am working for Susan Thomas, and I can get you back in," says Ryan.

"What's the catch, Ryan? You are not being nice to me because of your Christian faith," says Ejay.

"I want you to keep asking Leon Nguyen about constitutional concurrence. I want to see you drive him crazy," says Ryan.

The two men shake hands. "You pay for my drink. It's the least you could do," says Ryan.

Susan Thomas and Leon Nguyen finally have their first gubernatorial debate. The room is filled with media. Two of the most popular political figures in America are about to bump heads. Ejay is given entrance but not the ability to ask questions. He picks a spot among the press corps and takes a seat.

Brent Williams asks the first question. "Is climate change real, and how do you fix it?"

Mr. Nguyen responds, "I believe climate change is a real thing, but even if America could cut our carbon footprint, it would not change much because most of the pollution comes from Asia."

Susan Thomas responds, "As leaders of the free world, America must begin to tax the world for excess pollution."

The audience cheers at the first question, which previews a clash between two titans.

"The next question was chosen by social media. Is America involved in too many wars?" asks Brent Williams.

"America is once again a world leader, and it is important to eliminate certain threats," says Susan Thomas.

"Leaders use violence as a last resort. I would use influence and sanctions first," argues Mr. Nguyen.

"We have one more question before we take a break. There is a new emerging technology called constitutional concurrence. Artificial intelligence will examine all of your bills and budgets and publish the results of anything unfair or unconstitutional. If elected, would you use the new technology?" asks Brent Williams as he nods and smiles at Ejay Wade.

Brent Williams doesn't know Ejay Wade. In fact, they would be considered rivals. Ejay is part of small media, and Brent Williams works for a large media company.

"I would use the new technology because everything I do would be above board," says Susan Thomas.

"I would also use the new technology," says Leon Nguyen.

The crowd cheers as both candidates welcome the new technology.

The two take a break to use the bathroom and get some water. Brenda Flowergarden is at the debate to help her brother Ryan. She is recording a selfie-style video for social media when she picks up a conversation Susan is having with Ryan after she leaves the bathroom.

"I just said yes because it sounded cool. I'm not using constitutional concurrence," says Susan.

Susan is speedwalking and drying her hands. She fails to notice Brenda is in the restricted area recording.

The following day, someone else clips Brenda's live stream and it goes viral.

Susan marches into her office and walks up to Ryan's desk.

"Ms. Thomas, how can I help you?" asks Ryan.

Susan Thomas takes Ryan's laptop and slams it onto the floor.

"You stupid traitor, get the hell out of my office. Consider yourself fired. Tell your stupid sister she ruined my political career!" yells Susan.

Ryan looks surprised. He has no idea what happened until he opens his social media and sees the video.

Brenda is waiting for Ryan when he comes out of the office.

"Your fifteen minutes of fame just lost me my career," says Ryan.

"I was live streaming. I didn't know my microphone would pick that up. I didn't know she would come walking out of the bathroom. I saw you standing by and just started recording," says Brenda.

"For a genius, you're a real idiot," says Ryan.

Brenda stands there with tears in her eyes. She has dressed professionally for the first time in her life and wanted Ryan to notice her. She wipes her tears and quietly walks away.

Susan attempts to do damage control after Brenda's mistake hurts her chance of becoming Governor. The race is incredibly close.

Ryan drives to Susan's hotel. Her staff searches him before he can come in.

"I can help you win," says Ryan.

"You better make this good," says Susan.

"Use constitutional concurrence. You didn't understand the technology at first, but after a demo with the creator, you are on board. Then pull the creator to the side and tell him to take it easy on you," explains Ryan.

"Who is the creator?" asks Susan.

"Well, Ejay Wade is the owner. I don't know who created it for him. Maybe Mavin," says Ryan.

Susan walks up to Ryan and runs her fingers down his stomach.

"This is the last time you fail me. You may end up vanishing like Ethan," she says.

Ryan's body is frozen in fear.

"Oh God," he says as he realizes Susan is the dangerous one.

"You better pray to your God that this works, Ryan," says Susan.

Susan has her staff drive her to see Ejay Wade. He is standing outside drinking cranberry juice and watching the stars.

"Hello!" yells Susan with a fake smile.

Ejay just looks at her and then goes back to drinking his juice.

"I was confused. If you give me a second opportunity, I would love to introduce constitutional concurrence to the world," says Susan.

Ejay turns to her. "You're volunteering to use constitutional concurrence?" asks Ejay.

"Yes. If you will stand with me during a press conference to fix my image, I swear I will volunteer and use it," says Susan.

"I can't force you to do anything as Governor. But if you lie again, the world will know you are a dishonest person," says Ejay.

Susan shakes his hand. "I expect you at my office tomorrow," says Susan.

Ejay shows up and stands behind Susan Thomas as she explains that she was confused about the technology but is volunteering to use Artificial Intelligence Constitutional Concurrence.

After the meeting, Susan Thomas flies to see her old friend Farrah Muncheese in Florida. The two meet for a private dinner together.

"Can you get to Leon Nguyen and work your magic?" asks Susan.

"Don't call it magic. That's very racist," says Farrah. "So racist!" she continues.

"Listen, your political career is over. But I can promise you a position when I become Governor," says Susan.

"Nguyen does not like Black women," says Farrah.

"Do you know what he likes?" asks Susan.

"He likes technology," says Farrah.

"Can you catch him on a hot mic like they did me?" asks Susan.

"I can try to do some social engineering and find out his weakness," says Farrah.

The two shake hands.

Farrah catches a separate flight to South Carolina. Leon Nguyen decides to meet with her.

"The artificial intelligence clown did you in. What can I help you with?" asks Nguyen.

"I need a quiet job making six figures when you win," says Farrah.

"Why would I do that?" asks Nguyen.

She hands him a recording of the meeting she had with Susan Thomas. Leon Nguyen listens to it.

"I will give you a job after you use this to end her," says Nguyen.

"Me?" asks Farrah.

"You don't expect me to get dirty," says Leon Nguyen.

Farrah gets up and leaves.

The media is standing outside of the restaurant, ready to ask questions about why Farrah Muncheese has flown out to have dinner with Leon Nguyen. Mr. Nguyen steps out of the restaurant looking embarrassed.

"Listen, I took a meeting to help her. Nothing to see here," says Leon Nguyen.

Farrah looks shocked. You can tell she didn't call the meeting. Susan arranged for the media to be there. She knows she can no longer trust Farrah. She had to end her career.

In the coming weeks, both parties run a strong campaign. The people of South Carolina begin to view it as the lesser of two evils because both candidates are now tarnished.

A new social media video is posted of Clone Farrah Muncheese. She is still wearing a red nose and white gloves.

"I met with Leon Nguyen to try to get a job. After all, I have used my beauty and my body for years to get ahead. Can you blame me? I have to buy a third Mercedes-Benz. I am even connected to minors under 16 from Venezuela being caught working on cannabis farms in Florida," says Clone Farrah.

The real Farrah Muncheese watches with fear on her face. She runs upstairs and begins to pack her bags when she hears police sirens coming for her.

The police knock on the doors of Farrah's large home with an arrest warrant. Senator Scott Rippleton, who was arrested two years ago, turns on Farrah to cut his sentence down.

Farrah is placed in handcuffs. She puts her head down in shame as they place her in the police car. Farrah looks at her large home as they drive her away to jail for processing.

The blowback from the arrest of Farrah and Scott Rippleton two years earlier makes people look at Leon Nguyen with suspicion. He loses the election, and Susan Thomas becomes Governor of South Carolina.

Susan celebrates as the election numbers come in big. Ryan watches from a distance because he is still fired. Brenda walks up and holds his hand. He hugs his sister.

"I love you, sister, but I can't hire you for temporary work anymore," says Ryan.

She nods her head. "I know," she says.

Susan stands and gives her speech.

"I am the first Governor to introduce Artificial Intelligence Constitutional Concurrence. I am the most honest politician in the world," says Susan.

Ejay Wade's eyes light up as he watches her on television. He thinks that she was lying to him, but she keeps her promise.

Susan drives to her giant private suite to celebrate with her husband, Amir Bala. He brings her into the bedroom blindfolded.

"Did you get me a cake?" asks Susan.

A voice responds, "No, something better."

Veronica Moorchester is waiting for her in custom-made army-colored lingerie.

"Are you going to join in?" Susan asks Amir.

Ryan packs his things and drives back home to Georgia to decide what his next move is going to be. He comes to a halt on the road and watches a slow turtle crawl across the street. He finally makes it back to Georgia and stops by to see his father. Mr. Flowergarden brings out some milk and cookies.

"Watch your sister's back. You know she has trouble keeping a job," says Mr. Flowergarden.

"You're not sleeping with your assistant, are you, Dad?" asks Ryan.

"I have been faithful to your mother. I only cheated one time. Are you going to hold that against me forever?" asks Mr. Flowergarden.

"She has been around for a few years now, and I just want to make sure you didn't catch any feelings," says Ryan.

"Your room is still the way you left it. Your mother cleans it every week. You're welcome to spend the night," says Mr. Flowergarden.

"What am I supposed to do for a living?" asks Ryan.

"You have worked for crooked people your entire adulthood. Take that money and open a business. Hire your sister," replies Mr. Flowergarden.

"What kind of business?" asks Ryan.

"Rebecca has a book of cookie recipes. She still makes a mean red velvet cookie. Maybe you can take her on as a partner and open a bake shop," says Mr. Flowergarden.

"Dad, are you trying to make me a laughingstock in the world of politics?" asks Ryan.

"You already know you are going to run for City Council. You don't need my blessing, son. Go and run for City Council," says Ryan's father.

Ryan hugs his father and then leaves. His father shakes his head. Ryan couldn't shake his political thirst.

Farrah takes a deal for less time and is sent to a women's prison in Mississippi. When she arrives, the women are catcalling her. Farrah is stripped of her usual makeup and hair extensions.

She sits in her cell, which will be her home for the next five to seven years. Farrah cries into her pillow.

Mavin is given the privilege to order books on technology and artificial intelligence. He wants to know where he went wrong. He still has years to go on his prison sentence. He is hoping to form his own tech startup once he has finished paying his debt to society.

He finally understands he isn't getting out early. The warden is going to make sure he serves all ten years. Mavin becomes a problem solver, so the inmates never give him any trouble. He can answer questions on almost any subject.

Mavin has a doctorate degree but never calls himself Doctor. As arrogant as he is, that is the one thing he doesn't agree with. He doesn't even add "Ph.D." to his name. He believes in education for the sake of learning only.

Brenda goes back to streaming video games for her fans. She often dresses up in rainbow colors or as a cat. She loves to cosplay different characters, and she often goes to Comic-Con to meet fans.

Brenda knows she is attractive, hides the fact that she is a genius, and spends her money as fast as she can make it.

Ejay hands the program for constitutional concurrence over to Susan Thomas.

"Who made the program?" asks Susan.

"I came up with the concept, and my people helped me create it," says Ejay Wade.

"Who are your people?" asks Susan as she becomes irritated.

"My people," repeats Ejay.

Susan takes the program and downloads it. She loves the fact that it can break down complex laws. Susan is staring into the future.

Susan catches a private plane to an undisclosed location. When she arrives, some of the most powerful people in America are there. Her husband, Amir Bala, is already at the location and is invited because he is wealthy. Veronica Moorchester is invited, but she only has a limited invitation as a representative.

Leon Nguyen is present. He frowns when he sees Susan and whispers something in the ear of his assistant. He is still upset about the election.

Ramsey Finch Ox is present. He is serving breakfast like an employee as people arrive.

Ramsey Finch Ox finishes serving breakfast and then changes his clothing. He comes out on stage with deer antlers on his head in the shape of a crown.

"Ladies and gentlemen, welcome to our annual getaway. For some of you, this will be your first time. We ask that whatever you see here stay here. You must earn our trust. Welcome to our ceremony host, Vice President Sandman," says Ramsey Finch Ox.

The men and women run around outside in the cold with nothing but their undergarments. They laugh and run up and hit each other.

"Ouch!" yells Susan as Leon Nguyen slaps her on the back and yells congratulations.

Next, the group sits around in a circle and passes around wine in a fake skull purchased from a Halloween store. Susan enjoys some wine and passes the fake skull to Veronica Moorchester.

After the first night, Veronica and Susan have a private chat in her room.

"It feels weird. We are finally here, right? No reporters taking pictures of us, just peace and quiet. We don't even have our cell phones," says Veronica.

"Well, I will only be doing this once. I don't want to go to annual retreats," says Susan.

Veronica rolls up some marijuana and smokes it.

"You're a pothead now?" asks Susan.

Veronica offers her a hit. Susan joins in.

"Help me find my Rolex. I think housekeeping took it," says Susan.

They search all over her room for the lost watch.

"Are we ever going to talk about a future?" asks Veronica.

"I don't want to talk until 3 a.m. about the future tonight. We have a big day ahead of us," says Susan.

The following day, Vice President Sandman speaks to everyone.

"With the rise of Artificial Intelligence, do not get caught with your pants down like Farrah and Rippleton. If you have anything out in the open that can be discovered if it is public knowledge artificial intelligence can find it. These are dangerous times for powerful people," says Vice President Sandman.

He does not participate in the fun or games. The Vice President gives his speech and then gets into a helicopter. Once the Vice President leaves, they break out into a drinking game again. They begin singing a song.

"Freedom! We protect freedom!

Politicians! Who really needs them!

We sip our wine and we count our pensions, And they blame us when something's missing."

The members stand inside a room with a feast prepared. They have all the best food you could imagine. Mack Tuckerson gives a toast to Susan, who has just become Governor. They eat and enjoy the meal. Then Mack stands up again with a smirk.

"Our new Governor and her travel friend, Representative Moorchester, will now close out this lovely occasion by cleaning all this mess up," says Mack.

All the senior men and women laugh as they hand Susan Thomas and Veronica Moorchester a broom and mop.

"Before you get on that plane, Governor, you will have this place spotless. This will prove that you are never above humanity," says Mack Tuckerson. He was anti artificial intelligence.

The influence of Clone Mavin has grown within the clone world, mostly left dormant after Ryan destroyed the backup computer. The clone still exists on a drive somewhere. Did Lawrence and Joshua create a backup drive? Clone Mavin is now giving orders to all the other clones.

Mack Tuckerson finishes his morning run on the treadmill. Every morning, he works out and then grabs some coffee. He checks his emails when he sees he was tagged in a social media post.

"My name is Clone Mack Tuckerson. I voted and fought to allow a halfway house for sex offenders to be put near an elementary school. The plan eventually failed, but you must ask yourself why I agreed with it. This wasn't some harmless situation like when I pulled the fire alarm in college. Children could have been hurt," says Clone Mack Tuckerson.

The real Mack Tuckerson stares at the clown version of himself. He has the usual red nose and white gloves, but he is also wearing colorful circus pants. Clone Mack Tuckerson backs away from the screen and starts dancing in his clown pants.

"Son of a bitch!"

Mack Tuckerson calls a press conference.

"The creator of these new clones — because the original creator is in prison — is mocking me with racism. There are only two Black Senators right now, and he has me dancing a jig in clown pants. I am professional and educated. You may disagree with some of my votes, but to mock me and have me dancing like a clown is beyond the pale. I demand to know who is creating these clowns, and we will find you," says Mack Tuckerson.

Brent Williams raises his hand to ask a question.

"Wouldn't it be considered freedom of speech and a violation if the government goes after someone for mockery?" asks Brent Williams.

"Well, we will let the court decide," replies Mack.

A new video is published on social media. This time, over 100 clones are using balloons to float around Capitol Hill. Clone Mavin stays hidden in the shadows as the head clone. The clone of Mack Tuckerson is floating without a balloon, instead using his clown pants.

"Weeee!" yells Clone Mack Tuckerson.

The real Senator Mack Tuckerson is growing angry. A clone of Susan Thomas floats away with her balloon, using an ice cream cone as a microphone.

"I'm a Governor now! Who knows what I had to do to become Governor!" yells Clone Susan as she floats away with her red nose.

Veronica Moorchester pays a visit to Ryan on behalf of Susan. Ryan is preparing signs to run for city council.

"Where are the bots?" asks Veronica.

"I smashed the computer into pieces. There has to be a copycat unless they somehow saved the hard drive," says Ryan.

Veronica grabs Ryan's shirt. "Who is they?" she asks.

Ryan and Veronica pay a visit to Lawrence and Joshua to see if they still have the clones.

"You messed up my Forex money, and now you're accusing us?" asks Joshua.

"Someone is operating these clones. Did you make a copycat?" asks Ryan.

Lawrence points to the door and yells, "Get out!" to Ryan and Veronica.

Ryan and Veronica pace outside.

"I don't think it's them," says Ryan.

"Who do you think is doing it?" asks Veronica.

"Lawrence and Joshua only care about money. Mavin is the only person I know smart enough to pull this off," says Ryan.

"I will hire an expert to get to the bottom of this. There must be a signature somewhere," explains Veronica.

Veronica sends copies of the videos to a professional to see if they can find out who created the clones.

Veronica logs on and sees a new video being uploaded. The clone of Veronica is jogging on a track and wearing an Army jogging suit.

"Oh no!" yells Veronica at the computer.

"My name is Clone Veronica Moorchester, and I have been absent on most voting days since I became a member of Congress," says Clone Veronica.

The video cuts to Veronica carrying loads of running shoes out of a store.

"I spend most of my time shopping and working out. I am more interested in my fitness and my looks than being a good congressperson," says Clone Veronica.

Veronica Moorchester sits and looks at the screen in devastation. Her phone rings, but she ignores it instead of answering. Veronica's next reaction is to go running to cope with the stress, but she doesn't want to be seen in public. Instead, she sits on her bed and cries.

The following day, Veronica Moorchester uploads a response video.

"I am calling on Congress to create a law for responsibility and accountability for people using artificial intelligence," she says.

People begin to post comments asking if she would even show up for the vote. Veronica knows her political career is in danger.

Mavin is watching the news in prison. He recognizes the clones look like his, but he didn't create one of Veronica Moorchester. Someone copied his entire style of work.

The prison warden calls Mavin to his office.

"Sir, I promise these are not my clones. I have no idea who copied my style," says Mavin.

Warden James stands up and paces around the office. "Can you help find out who is creating them?" asks Warden James.

"Will you take some years off my sentence if I help?" asks Mavin.

"You killed a Senator," says the warden.

Mavin refuses to help and is placed back into his cell. He stares at the four walls, thinking, *Who could have copied my design?*

Clone Mavin is walking in a world he designed himself. He makes himself larger than all the other clones so that he can look down on them. His assistant, Clone Vice President Sandman, is dancing and clapping his hands as he walks behind Mavin.

Clone Mavin and Clone Vice President Sandman are not viewable to anyone except the clones. He remains shrouded in mystery and creates a zapper that can erase any clone at any time.

Clone Mavin stands in front of a building on Capitol Hill. He claps his hands and replaces the building with a circus tent.

A new video is uploaded, this time to several accounts. Artificial intelligence is becoming harder to trace because people are sharing the videos and multiple accounts are uploading them.

"My name is Clone Amir Bala, the First Gentleman of South Carolina. You rarely see us together because I constantly fly to Las Vegas to gamble and have V.I.P. parties," says Clone Amir.

The real Amir Bala laughs at the attempt at mockery, but he doesn't care if people know about his gambling habits because he is wealthy. However, Susan Thomas is concerned about the optics.

She calls her husband to her office in the Governor's Mansion.

"Can you invite your friends here and play poker in private?" asks Susan.

"My whole life I have been a free man. Now I am shackled by your success," says Amir.

"I give you everything you ask for! You get to sleep with whoever you want to. You get to spend all the money you can. I'm just asking you to be discreet," says Susan.

Amir Bala gives her a salute in anger. "Yes, Governor, I will follow your command," says Amir.

He storms out of her office and speeds up the street in his Corvette.

Susan Thomas needs land to build a new state park in South Carolina. She is running into problems with Artificial Intelligence Constitutional Concurrence because she plans on taking more land from the Gullah Geechee people of South Carolina, and her budget mostly benefits white people.

She calls Ejay Wade on the phone.

"Hey, this software has weird racial blocks built into it," says Susan.

"The software is designed to look at anything unfair in government, not just violations of certain articles and amendments," replies Ejay.

"I'm not a racist," says Susan.

"I didn't accuse you of being racist. You're a sitting Governor; you can do what you want," says Ejay.

Susan hangs up and then proceeds to override the suggestions made by artificial intelligence.

The following morning, she wakes up to her phone ringing. The system publishes to the world that Susan bypassed certain concerns and that her budget and land grab are unfair to Black residents of South Carolina.

"Why me?" yells Susan.

"If you remove the program, people will look at you as dishonest," says Amir Bala.

"Publish a response stating we are working on fixing glitches within the system," says Susan.

She has the program removed and then implements her plan, taking more land from the Gullah Geechee people and enforcing her unfair budget that puts 99 percent of resources in the hands of white people.

Susan goes and plays golf with a few of her friends. The nameless man from Washington, D.C., who has been watching her career for years, comes to visit.

"Why is a former Drug Czar worried about South Carolina?" asks Susan.

"You volunteered for Constitutional Concurrence. That puts everyone on the hook to have to follow it to a comma," says the nameless man.

"I stopped using the program. We will say it is broken and can't be fixed," says Susan.

The nameless man lights a cigar on the golf course and then walks off.

In the coming weeks, an outside program starts to publish a constitutional analysis and a report of all violations of the rule of law that Susan Thomas has ordered.

Susan decides to fly to Georgia to meet with Ejay personally. Ejay is working on a report of the Georgia school budgets.

"I hope you know your little trick may have cost me future voters," says Susan.

"You hope to become President someday," says Ejay.

"You made me look like a bigot," says Susan.

"Why did your actions cause more harm to Black people than white people? Elected officials still aren't tired of the unfair treatment. We are the easy targets," says Ejay.

"You are on a racial crusade and witch hunt, but I am not your enemy. Do I look like a member of the Klan?" asks Susan.

"What do you want? You dropped the program, so why are you here?" asks Ejay.

"Are you going to pretend like this new website mocking me isn't your work?" asks Susan.

She shows Ejay an Artificial Intelligence Constitutional Concurrence website that was published a few weeks earlier.

"I didn't create the website. It's a copycat," explains Ejay.

"We are still tracking down the person who copied the clown clones. God help you if we link any of this to you," says Susan.

"Hey, what I suggested was voluntary. The people you're angry at didn't care to ask for permission," says Ejay.

Clone Mavin finally makes himself visible to the public in an uploaded video.

"Four years ago, you imprisoned my creator. Today, we will make sure the people responsible pay. We are going to expose any unconstitutional action by any government official. We are going to read through every law and policy at every level. We are also going to expose any corporations that have been allowed to color outside of the lines. It is only right that we dress you in clown suits. You have turned America into a circus."

"Meet Ryan Flowergarden, the new city council person. He got his start working for Ethan Sipper, a scumbag. If you violate any laws, Mr. Ryan, we will publish them and let the world know.

Also, meet Amir Bala. He was given a large tax break because he promised to build something for Charleston, South Carolina, and he didn't deliver. Later, he married Susan Thomas, who became the Governor of South Carolina. His failure to deliver was never mentioned again. He gambles every month in Las Vegas."

Clone Mavin is wearing a prison jumpsuit in honor of his creator.

The real Mavin sits behind bars, nervous. He clearly isn't in control of the program, but someone is drawing heat to him. The program cannot just run on its own. What is going on out in the real world beyond the prison walls?

Clone Mavin and his clown squad comb through every law passed at every level of government going back to the founding of America. They do it in one week. Every Black Code and Jim Crow law passed locally is published. If it is available to the public, Robot Mavin and his clowns find it. Clone Mavin now also controls the Constitutional Concurrence program and applies it to every decision ever published by the Supreme Court.

Clone Mavin appears again.

"The United States Supreme Court was supposed to protect the rule of law. However, United States v. Cruikshank was the most unconstitutional decision ever made by our high court. The Colfax Massacre opened the door for mob rule against Black American citizens, and the 14th Amendment has been violated so many times that it makes me not even take the Supreme Court seriously."

"Ladies and gentlemen, I have created clown clones of the U.S. Supreme Court as well. We will also examine every decision and publish any violations of the rule of law by our courts. If you are bold enough to hurt citizens through crooked government, then the least we can do is let the world know."

Clone Mavin creates nine clone Supreme Court justices who also wear red noses and white gloves.

Chief Justice Snick picks up the phone and calls Vice President Sandman.

"Some kid is out here making a mockery of the Supreme Court. I would like to know who it is."

"Chief Justice Snick, we already know who it is. We can't say anything yet. They technically haven't broken any laws. We have a First Amendment issue," says Vice President Sandman.

"How did they know Farrah Muncheese committed a crime? They must be doing something illegal. Find the crime!" yells Justice Snick.

Vice President Sandman picks up the phone.

"If they do anything illegal, place them in handcuffs," says Vice President Sandman.

The nameless man on the other end of the phone responds, "If they break any laws, we will indict those idiots."

The nameless man pays another visit to Susan Thomas. He hands her a letter. She reads it and then places it in the shredder.

"I should have known. What took you so long to find out?" she asks.

"We found out quickly. Making a mockery of the government is not a crime. We can't do anything right now," says the nameless man.

"This isn't giving a President a big nose in a drawing. This dirtbag is examining everything we publish," says Susan.

"This person has no power other than making people laugh at us or hate us. You can still run your state the way you want," says the nameless man.

"I have a watchdog snitch telling on me!" says Susan.

"Follow the law," says the nameless man as he walks away.

Ryan Flowergarden goes to visit his father's church. He steps inside looking for his dad.

"Dad!" he yells.

Ryan's father is not in the main section, so Ryan heads back to the study room. Ryan sees his father coming out of the study room fixing his pants. Rebecca comes out next. Ryan can smell intercourse in the air and sees smeared lipstick on Rebecca's face.

Ryan punches his father in the face.

"What the hell, son!" yells Mr. Flowergarden.

"Councilman Flowergarden, I can explain," says Rebecca.

"You're cheating on my mom again!" yells Ryan.

"Your mother doesn't touch me anymore. She gave us permission as long as it's behind closed doors," says Mr. Flowergarden.

Ryan stops and thinks for a moment. He gets into his car and drives to his father's house to talk to his mom.

Ryan bursts through the door.

"Mom!" he yells.

His mother comes out of the kitchen. She can tell by the look on Ryan's face that he found out.

"You let him cheat!" yells Ryan.

"I can't make your father happy in that way anymore," says Ms. Flowergarden.

Ryan throws the red velvet cookies that are sitting on the table. His mother sinks down and begins to cry.

"Brenda understood," his mother says.

Ryan's whole world falls apart as he jumps in his car next to confront his sister Brenda. He arrives and bangs on her door, but nobody answers. Brenda is out jogging when she finally returns home and sees her brother's car driving away.

Susan is at her hotel in Atlanta, pacing back and forth. She has finally gotten a few gray hairs among her honey-colored strands. She sips on her vodka as her heart turns cold.

"Fuck this!" she says.

Susan drives to the home of the alleged person whose signature is all over the videos being uploaded, mocking her and the rest of the government. Susan knocks on the door a few times and then looks down at her Rolex. Her security waits patiently for her by her black SUV.

A young woman comes to the door dressed like a red ninja, but with her cleavage showing.

"Governor," she says in a nervous tone.

It is Brenda Flowergarden.

Susan pushes her aside and walks into her home.

"You're the one who's been mocking us?" asks Susan.

Brenda looks scared. Her heart is racing.

"Say something!" yells Susan.

"Governor, I want to show you something," says Brenda.

Brenda opens her laptop. She shows Governor Susan Thomas footage from a few years ago. She shows Susan and her men walking into a building. She fast-forwards it until Ethan Sipper walks into the same building. She shows Susan's men putting something large, rolled up in plastic, into the van and driving off. She shows Susan leaving the building, but not Ethan Sipper.

"You didn't have cameras inside the building, but Bob's Chicken Hut next door had outside cameras."

Susan is stunned.

"You can't prove anything," says Susan.

"I know, but I am going to continue to publish my findings, the things that I can prove. Everything that is public record," says Brenda.

"You stupid little brat. You sit in here dressed like a slutty ninja all day and mock me for the hard work I do as a government official. You set women back one hundred years," says Susan.

"I hope I don't mysteriously vanish like Ethan Sipper did," says Brenda.

Susan storms out and slams the door.

Flashback:

Ethan Sipper finds himself standing on plastic.

"No!" he yells as one of Susan's men hits him over the head and then throws a plastic bag over his head to suffocate him. They throw Ethan in the back of a van and drive off as Susan lights a cigar.

Brenda is next door monitoring the cameras she set up at the chicken restaurant. After the van drives off, Brenda follows it.

The Van stops after a few moments. Susan's men open the back of the van and let Ethan Sipper out.

"You guys could have gotten me out of there quicker!" yells Ethan.

"We had to make it look real," says one of Susan's men, as he counted the money handed to him in a large duffle bag.

Brenda drives up to meet them. Ethan gets in the car with her, and the two drive off.

Present Day:

After Susan storms out of Brenda's home, Ethan comes out of hiding.

"She sounded mad," says Ethan.

"She thinks she killed you," says Brenda.

"Listen, I'm lucky one of her men told me it was coming, or I would be dead. Our plan is almost complete," says Ethan.

Brenda tears up.

"I didn't think they would give Mavin ten years," she says.

"Listen to me, kid. He never respected you. You planted the idea to create clones. You would sneak in at night to fix his design. You loved him, and he didn't love you. You don't owe him," says Ethan.

"I know, but…" she replies.

"These men look down on you. Who gave Ryan the push to run for City Council?" asks Ethan.

Brenda thinks for a moment.

"Get ready. The grand reveal is coming, young lady," says Ethan.

Mavin is reading a book on quantum physics in prison when one of the inmates comes and gets him out of the library.

"Do you need help with math again?" asks Mavin.

The inmate responds, "No, your girl is on TV, bro."

Mavin fixes his glasses and walks into the TV room. He sees Brenda Flowergarden on the news.

"It has been revealed that the young lady who almost died in a car crash a few years ago hacked into the artificial intelligence to stop it. Brenda Flowergarden, the sister of Councilmember Ryan Flowergarden, graduated at the top of her class from the Massachusetts Institute of Technology," says Brent Williams.

Mavin looks surprised. How could a stupid girl like Brenda graduate from MIT? She is the one controlling his clone program.

Mavin gets mad and throws the book at the TV, and storms out. He walks up to the guard and demands to see the warden.

"I got set up. I'm innocent!" yells Mavin.

The guard punches Mavin in the stomach and then throws him in his cell.

Mavin is so intelligent that he figures out he was set up within seconds, but Brenda is even smarter. Brenda has an eidetic memory. She can look over Mavin's shoulder and see his code, wait for him to take a break, and then make corrections to his code.

The police storm Brenda's home. Ethan is nowhere to be found, but she is there. The police place her in handcuffs. Agent Morgan with the FBI walks in after the police.

"Finally, we got you on a cybercrime. Brenda Flowergarden, you have the right to remain silent. Anything you say can and will be used against you in a court of law. If you can't afford an attorney, one will be provided for you," says Agent Morgan.

"Looks like a witch hunt to me. Perhaps I wore the wrong costume today," says Brenda.

She is calm, as if she knows she is going to jail. The press is waiting outside as journalists reveal she is suspected of cybercrimes.

When Brenda arrives at the jail for processing, she is met by a large female guard with huge arms. She makes Brenda remove her clothing and tells her to squat and cough.

"Are you serious? That's so gross," says Brenda.

The guard just stares in anger until Brenda follows instructions.

They place Brenda in her cell as a high-profile inmate. The large guard comes to her cell and hands her a bag with her clothes.

"Someone posted bail for you pretty fast," says the guard.

The gamer community, who know Brenda as Gamer Girl 413, raises bail for her. The police confiscate all her hardware and software, but the gamer community starts creating their own clones as payback. They believe Brenda was arrested for speech.

Brenda arrives at her home. She pushes a bookshelf, which turns into a swing door revealing her secret room, untouched by the police. Ethan is there eating popcorn. He stands up and claps.

"Now, let's get you ready for court. You're going to beat this case," says Ethan.

Clone Mavin appears to the world.

"You arrested Gamer Girl 413. Now I am going to release all the racist restrictions built into housing covenants across America. The end is near, and all corruption shall be exposed."

Mavin unleashes millions of housing covenants created to prevent owners from selling their houses to Black Americans.

Brenda receives some pushback from the white supremacist community.

"She is a white girl! Why does she keep doing 'woke' stuff and releasing things done to Black people? She must like Black guys! I hate Gamer Girl 413," says one of the spectators.

A clear line is being drawn in the sand. Much of the corruption Brenda releases shows race at the center of it, but Brenda is white. She never considers herself a Republican or a Democrat and never uses phrases like "ally." Brenda doesn't even like talking about race. Nevertheless, the far right starts painting her as a Malcolm X–type character. They are upset that much of the corruption being exposed is race-related.

Clone Mavin uploads another video. He shows the salaries, net worth, and stock trades of every politician at every level. People begin to create trackers online and copy the trades of members of Congress.

Veronica Moorchester's net worth is now over two million dollars. Veronica watches from home as people begin to copy her stock trades and accuse her of insider trading.

"What did I do to her?" asks Veronica to her staff.

Brenda shows up to court. The head prosecutor is a hard-nosed type named Francis Montage. He meets with Brenda to try to get a plea agreement instead of going to trial.

"Young lady, you have caused a lot of trouble. I am offering you two years, and we want a public apology," says Francis.

"My client did not commit any cybercrimes. She merely published what was already made public to the world," says Jody Falen.

"How could she have known Farrah Muncheese or Rippleton committed crimes unless she hacked their computers?" argues Francis.

"Mavin Prep exposed Rippleton," says Jody Falen.

"Then Rippleton told on Farrah to shave years off his sentence," says Brenda.

"There has to be a crime somewhere in what you have released. I will find it!" says Francis.

"Wait, a brilliant lawyer like you would not go on a fishing expedition. What's going on, Francis?" asks Jody.

Francis smiles. He slaps a thick packet in front of Brenda.

"The Computer Fraud and Abuse Act. You hacked a car and lied and called it a miracle. That car never malfunctioned. You set it up to make it look that way to pretend you were not the mastermind you are…" says Francis. "Here is the funny part, the car was not fully remote. They secretly hire drivers in the Philippines to help steer the cars. You hacked them."

Brenda puts her head down.

"I'm going to prison," she says.

"We need a break," says Jody.

Brenda sat in the lobby, having a private chat with Jody.

"Tell me you're not the one who hacked the car!" says Jody.

"His team already found my signature. That's why I'm here. If he didn't have the smoking gun, I wouldn't be here," says Brenda.

Brenda and Jody Falen walk back into the office.

"I will take the deal for two years," says Brenda.

"Two? No, I mean five years," says Francis.

Brenda looks shocked.

"A genius who doesn't know law," says Francis.

Brenda gets up and gets ready to leave.

"If you walk out that door, make it ten years," says Francis.

Francis went from a pushover playing dumb to holding all the cards, and Brenda was headed to prison.

Ryan Flowergarden rushes from his job to support his sister. He makes it to the courthouse but is stopped by security.

Francis signals for them to let Ryan in.

"Too late. Your sister signed a deal. She is headed to a federal prison for five years. You can say goodbye," says Francis.

Ryan walks over and gives his sister a hug. She is placed in handcuffs and hauled off to processing. This time, she was headed to prison for real.

Governor Sarah Thomas was at her home in Georgia, taking a break from her governor duties in South Carolina. She had her own security team with her.

A messenger pulls up on a bike and delivers a phone to the governor.

"Listen carefully. Don't panic. We are going to have lunch," says Ethan Sipper.

Susan was shocked. She thought she had seen Ethan suffocated and dragged out of her building years ago. At first, she thought she was going crazy, or maybe it was a trick from artificial intelligence. People knew Ethan was missing, but the only people who should or would know he was dead were Sarah and the two men she was with that day.

She invites Ethan to have a meal with her. Her security searches him and lets him through.

Ethan has a seat in front of the governor. He appeared calm but was angry on the inside.

"Choose your words carefully, Ethan," warns Sarah.

"Brenda is very important to me. Here is what I need from you. Veronica Moorchester will be her handler. She will offer her a work program optimizing artificial intelligence for the government during her five-year sentence. After she serves her time, Veronica will make sure she is freed," says Ethan.

"If I deliver, then you and I are even," says Susan.

"You will never hear from me again. As much as I hate you, I don't want to look over my shoulder for the rest of my life," says Ethan.

"Who is she to you?" says Susan.

Flashback:

Ethan was sitting in his office, depressed. He had lost all of his influence, and things weren't working out as he planned.

Ryan's younger sister, Brenda, stops by to see Ryan.

"He's not here. He's out trying to pick up business," says Ethan.

"I know," says Brenda.

She hands Ethan files on her family, including herself.

"Add these to the collection of files," says Brenda.

Ethan opens the files. He sees nude photos of Brenda from when she was a cam girl.

"You want me to have dirt on you and your family?" asks Ethan.

"You trust me, and I trust you," says Brenda.

"You are going to be the girl who changes America," says Ethan Sipper.

Brenda's hand shook a little bit.

"Are you nervous?" asks Ethan.

"Yes. As a matter of fact, I am nervous," says Brenda.

"I told you I was a solid. If you trust me, you will have the power to fix America. You will no longer be a nobody," says Ethan. Ethan continues, "when I met you, that boy had destroyed your self-esteem. You cut yourself. Ryan kept it our secret. But I promised to be your mentor and protection, and no boy or man has harmed you since. Do I still have your trust?"

Brenda nods and then walks away. Ethan sits in his chair and lets it all sink in.

Brenda checked into federal prison, where she did not receive a decent welcome like Mavin. Some of the women were jealous of her looks.

Brenda's first breakfast didn't go so well. She stares at the food because it looks gross to her. She looks around and sees the other women frowning at her.

"Hey, Barbie, if you can't eat prison food, then don't bring your little pretty ass to prison!" a woman yells.

Representative Moorchester brings some regular clothing for Brenda to wear. The guards watch Brenda swap out her prison attire. They give her a stink look to show they disapproved of the favoritism.

"Before we leave…" says Veronica. Veronica throws a perfect punch to Brenda's face. "That's for ruining my political career, you dumb bitch!" yells Veronica.

They pick Brenda up from the floor and hand her a cloth to stop her nose from bleeding.

"I think you broke my nose," says Brenda.

"Get your skinny ass in the car," says Veronica.

Veronica drives Brenda to the Federal Building, where she will be working for the good of the government.

"I am sorry for what I did to you. It wasn't personal," says Brenda.

Veronica points to the desk where Brenda will be sitting.

"First, they want you to look at the budget and identify waste, fraud, and abuse."

"Can I have breakfast first?" asks Brenda.

"Didn't they feed you in prison?" asks Veronica.

"No," says Brenda.

Veronica knows she is lying but sends a mailboy to get her whatever she wants for breakfast. Brenda comes from an old-fashioned country family, so she eats bacon, eggs, grits, toast, and waffles. Veronica, who has to watch her figure, watches Brenda eat with jealousy in her heart.

"Now, start working on the budget."

Brenda uses technology to comb through the budget and identify waste.

"There is a lot of money going to daycares in Minnesota, but when I look up the businesses, it seems like there is no activity. Also, there is a ton of money being missed when auditing defense."

"Ignore the defense budget and send me the information on Minnesota," says Veronica.

Brenda does as she is told.

"Also, I removed the artificial intelligence clone of you, Veronica. She is on this drive. If you want to destroy it, you can," says Brenda.

Brenda hands Veronica a flash drive. Veronica puts it in her pocket.

"Thanks," says Veronica.

Veronica calls Vice President Sandman.

"She found over a trillion dollars in waste," says Veronica.

"Good. Before you do anything, send me the files on all the waste she found. You may have a career in the future," says Vice President Sandman.

Mavin is invited out of his cell. The fellow prisoners trade some snacks to get Mavin a cake. He has knocked out five years of his prison sentence.

One of the inmates stands up.

"Mavin did five years standing on his head, and he will make it five more years," says the inmate.

The fellow inmates clap and bring Mavin a cake. He becomes known as the advice giver while in prison. His arrogance fades, and he finds joy in helping people solve their problems.

Ryan Flowergarden is sitting in his office when he is paid a visit.

"My son is a City Council member. I am very proud," says Ms. Flowergarden.

"Mom, what brings you to Atlanta?" asks Ryan.

"I just wanted to check on you, make sure you're eating," says Ms. Flowergarden.

"You came to ask if I will forgive Dad," says Ryan.

"Rain, you're a grown man now. You can do whatever you want. But I can't give your father what he wants any longer. I live my life for me now. I'm glad Rebecca makes him happy," says Ms. Flowergarden.

"You guys are making a mockery of marriage," says Ryan.

"We are getting divorced. Your father left me the big house. He is moving out," says Ms. Flowergarden.

Ryan's eyes tear up.

"I will never forgive him!" says Ryan.

"Your father is also stepping down as pastor. He said he can't lead the flock if he can't lead by example," says Ms. Flowergarden.

Ryan grows cold.

"Take care of your sister. She is going to need you when she is released from prison. I am going to travel to California for a while," says Ms. Flowergarden.

"What about the house? Are you going to leave it sitting?" asks Ryan.

"Rain, your daddy purchased that house for you and Brenda originally. He worked his whole life for you. Anyway, I love you, and I will be back in a year," says Ms. Flowergarden.

She gives her son a hug and then steps back and looks at his face. Ryan looks exactly like his father.

Mack Tuckerson pays a visit to Veronica and Brenda.

"Mack wants his clone as well. Remove the clown nose, transfer it to a hard drive, and give it to Mack," says Veronica.

"Are you going to make me give every clone away to Congress?" asks Brenda.

"You destroyed my career. You are going to help me fix it. Every member of Congress who wants their clone can stop by and get their clone. Your stupid clone protocol is done," says Veronica.

"You didn't say you were going to destroy my life's work in the process," says Brenda.

Veronica holds her hand out. Brenda hands her a removable hard drive for Mack Tuckerson.

"Baby girl, when you run for the Senate, let me know. I will throw my weight behind you," says Mack.

He frowns at Brenda and then leaves.

"This is so embarrassing," says Brenda.

"You started it. Now you want to cry like a victim. Put your big-girl panties on. Stop crying before I make you mop floors," says Veronica.

They place Brenda back in handcuffs and escort her to the van with her head down.

The following day, Ryan Flowergarden pays a visit to the Federal Building to ask Veronica if he can see his sister.

"Come in. I'll grab her," says Veronica.

Brenda enters the office for a supervised visit.

"Are they treating you decent?" asks Ryan.

"My big brother, you wait until now to come see me?" asks Brenda.

"You knew Dad was cheating and leaving Mom, and you kept it from me. You're lucky I decided to visit you," says Ryan.

"Mom made me promise. It doesn't matter now anyway. Everything is gone. You and Dad were supposed to protect us!" yells Brenda.

"How? You kept me in the dark. My little sister, a criminal mastermind. You're a regular Pinky and the Brain," says Ryan.

"What? Who is that?" asks Brenda.

Ryan frowns at his sister, who is too young to understand the reference.

"When you are freed, I am moving you to California. We are leaving the South," says Ryan.

Brenda stands up.

"You can't save me, Ryan. I am permanently on the government's shit list," says Brenda.

She doesn't attempt to hug or touch her brother. She just walks away in sadness.

Ryan walks to the restroom before leaving the building. He breaks down, and his eyes are filled with tears as he watches the girl he held as a baby in a prison program.

Ryan walks into his City Council office, sits down, and stares.

Ethan Sipper attends a college graduation event at Harvard University. Some of the brightest minds on the planet are about to take a leap into the real world.

He approaches a young lady who wears the mark of a top graduate.

"Casey Glore?" Ethan asks.

"Yes, that's me," the young lady responds.

"Are you ready to save America?" asks Ethan Sipper.

The young lady looks confused.

Brenda continues her good work and follows the orders of Veronica Moorchester. Members of Congress show up one by one over time to take possession of the clones Mavin and Brenda created.

Brenda is escorted back to the women's prison at night and placed in her cell. She has her own room for protection. She lies down and cries until she falls asleep.

Susan rises to power at the annual government retreat function. She is now wearing the deer-antler crown on her head. She stands before the other members.

"As Governor of the great state of South Carolina, I want to welcome you all to a feast! We have watched Veronica Moorchester grow over the years, and now, with her help, we will optimize government," says Susan.

The members stand and applaud.

"The stupid Clown Assembly that used to mock us has been destroyed. The little girl who challenged us is now behind bars. She didn't understand patriotism, but we do," says Susan.

She raises her wine glass as the most powerful people in America sip wine and sing together.

Mavin works out and then hits the shower. Afterwards, he sits in his cell and studies. Mavin focuses on self-improvement and wonders where he went wrong. How could he be a better man? Did he allow his arrogance to ruin him? He had been praised his entire life and failed to see the blind spot.

Farrah Muncheese sits in her prison cell. The guards bring her mail stating her appeal has been denied. She trades away some of her money to get her own makeup in prison.

Farrah puts on her makeup and looks at her beautiful face in the mirror. She sends some money home to her cousin, who invests in Jamaican Black Castor Oil and coconut oil. They use Farrah's face as a wrongfully imprisoned woman and create a skincare line for the family.

The money that Farrah invests from prison starts to make her even more money. Farrah is becoming a multi-millionaire from behind bars.

Former Vice President Sandman becomes President after President Chandler dies from medical complications. He does a decent job but is not as popular as President Chandler.

President Sandman goes on camera to speak to the world.

"Ladies and gentlemen, we are no longer afraid of artificial intelligence. We will work with it. I give you America 2.0," says President Sandman.

Everyone counts down as they enter a new age of American prosperity and glory.

Veronica Moorchester receives a reward from the President of the United States for her work with Brenda.

Brenda is quietly ushered back into her cell. The guard leaves the door open and walks away for a moment.

"Hey!" yells Brenda.

Two inmates walk in and beat Brenda until she is lying on the floor bleeding. One of the inmates pulls down her pants and urinates on Brenda. The prison guard comes back.

"Clean this cell up, you smell like piss," says the guard. They closed the doors and locked Brenda in.

The End of Act Two

HUMANITY OPTIMIZED

A group of men sat around a table in Southwest Atlanta, counting their profits, when a loud rumble shook the street outside.

"Hey, you hear that?" Jordan asks.

The room fell silent. One of the men crept toward the window and peeled back the blinds.

A massive construction vehicle barreled into the side of the house.

Wood and drywall exploded inward. The men dove for cover as police officers poured through the opening.

Jordan's ears rang from the impact as he staggered to his feet.

An officer stepped forward and smashed the butt of his assault rifle across Jordan's face, sending him back to the floor. Another officer swung a sledgehammer through the dining room wall.

Behind the drywall there were stacks of cash wrapped in plastic. Rows of it. Enough to fill the room.

Mayor Ryan Flowergarden stood at a press conference hours later, eager to show the city his administration was serious about reducing crime in Atlanta.

Drugs and confiscated money were laid neatly across a long table for the cameras.

"My administration has lowered crime in Atlanta by ten percent," Ryan said. "Your children will be safer walking to school. The streets will be quieter at night. We now use technology to pinpoint gunshots and track stolen vehicles more efficiently. Every process has improved thanks to innovations developed by my sister, Brenda Flowergarden."

Brent Williams paced inside his newsroom, agitation written across his face.

"They didn't have to strike that young man in the face with a gun," Brent snapped.

"What's new?" Ejay replied calmly.

"Can you talk to Ryan? You two used to be close, right?"

Ejay shook his head. "Ryan don't fuck with us anymore. He only speaks to major outlets."

"Ever since he became mayor and that snake Ethan showed back up Ryan forgot about the people," Brent said.

Ejay leaned back. "You've worked in media as long as I have. You know we haven't trusted politicians since the *Tilden or Blood* campaign. I never trusted Ryan. You should've prepared yourself."

Ethan Sipper entered the mayor's office without knocking.

"People are still complaining about that officer hitting the kid with his rifle," Ethan said. "You need to suspend him."

Ryan turned slowly. "You want me to risk angering the police union?"

"If you don't act, the Blacks will explode," Ethan replied. "You can't keep playing neutral. Pick a side."

Brenda rode aboard her private train, which stopped only for fuel. A personal chef prepared her meals. Security lined each car.

They called her the Forecaster of America, a title earned through her work in artificial intelligence.

Veronica Moorchester, head of security and former member of Congress, disliked trains but loved control.

"Are you going to hold a press conference about your little experiment yesterday?" Veronica asks.

"That's not how the scientific method works," Brenda replied. "We need repeated testing to ensure it wasn't a fluke."

Veronica grabbed an apple from a silver fruit dish. "I knew that. Just keeping you sharp."

The train roared forward.

The only clown clone Brenda still owned was one of herself. She kept it as a reminder. A mirror. A sounding board.

"Are you ready to reveal your food optimization plan?" Clone Brenda asks. "I can draft the speech, or we can send the findings directly to President Thomas."

"Send it encrypted. Eyes only," Brenda ordered.

President Susan Thomas received the proposal and immediately reached for her secure line.

"Kid… tell me you're joking," Susan said when Brenda answered.

"This is optimization," Brenda replied evenly. "We anticipated trade-offs. My plan allocates food differently based on wealth, race, age, health status, etc… "

Susan cut in. "Stop being robotic. I need something that preserves stability."

Brenda stepped into her private office.

"You promised equality when you ran," Brenda said.

"This isn't equality," Susan shouted.

"Well, you're going to rip apart my optimization plan and then make me fall on my sword when people get upset." Says Brenda.

"You haven't been a prisoner for years. You are welcome to get off my train and go back to living your boring life as a cam girl, showing strangers your boobs for money." Says Susan.

Brenda hangs up on the President of the United States in anger.

Veronica Moorchester was standing guard at the door.

"Listen, you two had your thing in the past. Is she really a jerk all the time?" asks Brenda.

Veronica sighs.

"President Thomas can be demanding. Let's not forget our place." She reminds Brenda.

Brenda is focused on fixing her plan to feed America. She needed it to be acceptable to President Susan Thomas before it could be rolled out. Susan Thomas, being more on the conservative side, didn't want to cause a stir with the plan. The hang up was what exactly does it mean to be equal?

"Twin," Brenda says to her clone. "Create a model where everyone in America gets two thousand dollars per month based on the profits made from artificial intelligence productivity in America."

"Are you sure, you will be giving poor people and billionaires the same number of resources," says Clone Brenda.

Brenda's eyes tear up. "I'm fucking sure!"

Brenda closes her door and breaks down crying. Her plan to save the world was falling apart.

After Brenda's nap, she comes out of her office to eat her favorite food, chili. The chef delivered some of the best chili Brenda had ever tasted. However, the chili was more spicey than usual.

Veronica Moorchester calls the chef over to have him taste the chili himself.

"You know Brenda hates spicey food. Taste this." Says Veronica.

The chef refuses to taste the chili. He had a scared look on his face.

Veronica's eyes grow big. "Drop the spoon!" she yells to Brenda.

Veronica quickly pulls her side arm as the chef attempts to stab her with his knife. The two fight and tussle as Brenda falls on the ground, suffering from the poison. The chef and Veronica lose their weapons as the train speeds along.

They both dive for Veronica's gun. Veronica has enough and wraps her enormous legs around the chef's neck. She squeezes and then grabs a hold of a pipe for leverage. Veronica finally twists and you could hear the chef's neck snap.

Veronica runs to grab a special pen Brenda designed to treat poison. She looks into Brenda's eyes to see what color they were changing. Brenda points to the correct pen for Veronica before passing out. Veronica switches pens and then jabs Brenda in the chest as hard as she can with the antidote.

"Don't you die on me!" yells Veronica.

Brenda jumps back up in pain from being stabbed in the chest with the pen. She had to fight to catch her breath.

"Joe tried to kill me. Why?" she asks.

Susan calls Veronica's phone to check on Brenda. She's worried after a member of the security department informed her about the attack.

"Veronica, I need to see Brenda and her team. Tell her I want to see her real team," says President Susan Thomas.

President Susan Thomas sends helicopters to gather Brenda Flowergarden's team, which includes Ethan Sipper and Ejay Wade.

Ethan, Ejay, Veronica, and Brenda sit in the Oval Office, sweating bullets. They had all met Susan before, but this was a more powerful Susan. You could feel that she was now confident in her ability to lead.

Veronica looks at Ethan and Ejay.

"Your team is Ethan Sipper and Ejay Wade?" she asks, confused.

Susan addresses everyone.

"My security team helped me figure it out. Ethan Sipper recruited you when you were young and used you as his worker. Mavin was an unnecessary casualty because he figured something out. Ejay came up with Constitutional Concurrence, but he wasn't computer savvy, so Brenda built the program for him. You've all been playing us for fools."

Brenda looks down.

"Stop me when I tell a lie," Susan says.

Ethan remains silent, but rage burns behind his eyes. Susan's failed attempt on his life was not forgotten.

"I need to know why our artificial intelligence models keep failing. What did we get wrong?" Susan asks.

Ejay Wade raises his hand.

"What is this, middle school?" Susan snaps.

"Your models take power away from the American people. Artificial Intelligence can't understand Americans. Americans hate to comply. It's not American. Constitutional Concurrence was my last-ditch effort to align us," Ejay says.

"Did Mavin try to stop it?" Susan asks.

"Mavin was a fluke. The senator really died of a heart attack. They locked Mavin up because a senator died," says Ejay.

"Every model predicts the same outcome. When white-collar jobs vanish, American nationalism rises. They will elect someone more radical. All roads lead to the abolition of Immigration into America." Says Brenda.

"America is a nation of immigrants!" Susan says.

"Large white-collar corporations will cut the American labor force by eighty percent," Ejay says. "Americans will turn on blue-collar corporations. The country will go back to small-town USA… small, blue-collar businesses. They won't work for less, and they won't allow corporations to import cheap labor from other countries."

"How can they stop us? I am the President of the United States," Susan says.

"You are… but elections are coming," Brenda replies.

"They're going to run on abolishing USCIS," Susan predicts.

"Every model we run ends the same way," Brenda says. "Someone rises out of nowhere and abolishes USCIS."

Susan's face drains of color.

"Oh my God… they're going to elect an outsider."

Mack Tuckerson enjoyed lunch at his favorite café. People called him the Lion of the Senate because he was so popular, one of the few Black American senators still standing. He was tough, respected, and deep down carried a hatred for Republicans and Democrats.

Mavin walks into the café in jogging clothes and sits in front of Mack.

"Mack Tuckerson, I need your help."

"What are you doing, Mavin Prep?" asks Mack.

"You know who I am," Mavin responds.

"You killed a member of the U.S. Senate. We all know you," says Mack.

"I didn't mean to kill anyone. It was a prank. I was young," says Mavin.

Mack Tuckerson's patience begins to run out.

"Kid, what do you want?" asks Mack.

Mavin pulls out his laptop and sets it on the café table.

"Every model we ran triggered the end of immigration into America. I think one of my partners set me up," says Mavin.

Mack rolls his eyes.

"Okay, I'm not asking you to care about me. I can help you become president. If Susan Thomas runs for reelection, you can beat her if I help you," says Mavin.

Mack Tuckerson thinks for a moment. He knew Susan. She was once his junior, so he didn't exactly like the fact that she passed him up. Mack was smart but played the fool in order to get other members to drop their guard around him. He was the lovable, funny Black man.

"Why don't you run, Mr. Genius?" asks Mack.

"I'm not worthy. But when you were young, you took a picture with my father. You two were wearing those funny hats. He said you were a good man," says Mavin.

"Senator Prep. You're his son…the little boy we used to throw candy to. The hats are what we call a fez," says Mack.

"I need a job. Behind the scenes. But I can help you save America," says Mavin.

Mack Tuckerson thinks for a moment. "What about Brenda Flowergarden?" he asks.

"They have her. She is no longer Brenda Flowergarden. She thinks she can steer this ship. She thinks she can stop the inevitable," says Mavin.

Brenda Flowergarden was working day and night. She was running different models to see if she could save Immigration. Every model failed. Large corporations were building data centers all over and quickly firing Americans from their jobs. Americans would then see people coming into America by the millions for work. It was inevitable. If they couldn't stop greed on one end, they could damn sure stop it on the other end.

Casey Glore was a failed prodigy of Ethan Sipper. She started her own organization. She was against data centers being built in her community. Casey had become the embodiment of what Brenda could have been. The dark side. The other side of the coin.

Casey was driving a truck with several men in the back. They were dressed like clowns. She approached the gate of one of the data centers and then rams it at full speed. Casey approaches one of the cooling stations. She attaches a bomb to it and then gets in the truck and drives off. The bomb blows, dumping water all over the place.

Brenda decided to take a break. She was enjoying her favorite meal onboard the train when Veronica came with the bad news.

"These idiots are blowing up data centers now," says Veronica.

"That's not going to stop anything. This is misplaced anger," says Brenda.

Veronica turns on the news for her to see.

Brenda was staring at the younger version of her. In her eyes there was fire and the power of belief. This young lady was dangerous. Her followers had grown tired of the massive amount of water being used at data centers.

"We have to stop her!" yells Brenda.

"You have to finish your plan. I will call my friends at the FBI to stop her," says Veronica.

Brenda begins to worry, even though Veronica was making phone calls. She initiated a program called Humanity Optimized.

Brenda's systems go into protection mode. Brenda goes and secretly packs a bag. When the train stops to refuel, Brenda sneaks off the train and gets in a car driven by Ethan Sipper.

Veronica frantically searches for Brenda as the train pulls off. She calls Brenda's phone.

"Tell me you didn't get off the train!" yells Veronica.

"I know what I have to do. I started this and I have to be the one to finish it," says Brenda.

"This is bigger than you! You can't turn an aircraft carrier on a dime!" yells Veronica.

Brenda hangs up and tells Ethan to drive.

"Casey was supposed to be your replacement. I recruited her. She is smart but dangerous. She started her own movement called 316." Says Ethan.

"What does 316 mean?" asks Brenda.

"She thinks she is the savior of mankind. John 3:16," says Ethan.

Brenda rolls her eyes.

"You didn't think to call the authorities or to call me?" asks Brenda. "You just let a psycho clown girl take over!" she yells.

Mavin powered up his computer. His clone appears. "Clone Mavin, can we reduce Immigration levels without abolishing Immigration?" asks Mavin. Clone Mavin begins to run different models. Mavin goes for a jog while the system processes the information.

Dr. Bellamy had gone back to being a pastor. He decided to visit a Baptist convention in Atlanta to spread his message on the evil of artificial intelligence.

"These data centers are depriving us of water and Americans are losing their livelihoods in the name of innovation. These are serious times. We do not have time for Hip Hop, twerking and lazy African Americans with the sagging pants and gold teeth."

A man finally gets fed up with Dr. Bellamy's rhetoric from the crowd.

"Hey! I just lost my job to artificial intelligence. Now I have to come to church and hear this anti-black shit?" the man yells.

"I am merely showing you that African Americans need to fix themselves," says Dr. Bellamy.

A few people who were listening to the lecture decided to get up and leave. Something changed. Dr. Bellamy was able to voice his opinion of "lazy black people" in the past because everyone was busy working and paying bills. But Americans were starting to be terminated from their jobs due to the rise of artificial intelligence.

A man sticks a middle finger at Dr. Bellamy and walks out.

Dr. Bellamy was walking to his car after service talking on his phone to his wife.

"They keep calling me brother! I am not their brother. I want them to do better," says Dr. Bellamy.

The man who had walked out of the church walks up and knocks Dr. Bellamy out with one punch. He kicks Dr. Bellamy as he lies unconscious and then walks off.

"Go home you fucking Tether!"

Mavin returns from his morning run. He was in great shape because he worked out so much in prison. He enjoyed some grapes as he looked at the results of his request. The artificial intelligence saved Immigration but reduced levels to 10 percent for extreme cases and family unity only.

Mavin calls Mack Tuckerson on his cell phone.

"We can save Immigration by reducing levels to 10 percent. Extreme cases and family unity will be the exception," says Mavin.

Mack Tuckerson thinks for a minute.

"You knew I would agree, how?" asks Mack.

"Black Americans have a big heart and care about others; Politicians however misuse and abuse systems all the time. They abused the Immigration system, sometimes to the determent of Black Americans," Says Mavin.

Mack waits a moment before he responds.

"I need you to prepare me to crush Susan and Leon Nguyen in future debates. They are the only two people who can beat me," says Mack.

"Clone Mavin, we need a plan to make Mack Tuckerson President of the United States," orders Mavin.

"It's funny, I thought you didn't like black people. Why are you helping me?" asks Mack.

"I don't care about race. In prison, they treated all of us like shit. The funny part is the black people treated me like a human. Most of the prisons are segregated, but they put me near the black population in hopes that they would harm me. They didn't. They helped me. It's time to become one America," Says Mavin.

"Man, you're alright, I don't care what they say about you," says Mack.

Susan met with her White House staff to review intelligence gathered on Casey Glore and her movement. They were targeting data centers. There was also the problem of Brenda Flowergarden leaving the train, Brenda's clone named Twin was running the show and a rise in nationalism was on the way in America.

"We need to put our own information out there to keep the American people calm. We need to let them know everything is under control," says Susan.

One of the staff members responds.

"Madam President, the word control is polling horribly with Americans right now. Trust is eroding."

Casey Glore steps into her secret hideaway. She had armed men set up at the doors for protection. She had maps laid out of the different data centers she wanted to disrupt. Casey was dressed in tactical gear but was still wearing clown face paint. She turns on the television to see if she made the news.

"Americans have boycotted one of our favorite chicken brands for hiring migrant labor. If things don't turn around soon the price of chicken may go up," says the reporter.

The artificial intelligence prediction was beginning to come true. The fewer jobs' Americans had, the more they leaned towards nationalism and nationalist voices. Shock jocks took to the air waves to condemn mass migration while Americans were hurting for jobs.

The media approaches Mack Tuckerson as he attempts to go into his office.

"Senator, are you working on a plan with President Susan Thomas to combat this rise in nationalism?"

"No, it's inevitable. Americans don't want to see someone who is not American profit if they aren't given opportunities themselves," says Mack.

Susan sees the footage and calls Mack Tuckerson from the White House. They hadn't spoken since she became president.

"You son of a bitch. Are you planning a run for the White House?" she asks

"You are standing in the way of a fast-moving train Susan. We need to get out in front of this," says Mack.

"Well, enjoy your run. When I get reelected, I will see you again. Mack, we will meet again after I get into my second term," warns Susan.

Mack hangs up the phone on her.

Susan Thomas calls her press secretary into her office.

"Listen, Mack Tuckerson is planning a run for the White House next term. I want you to get a smaller newspaper to plant a story about him. I want them to call him a sale out and an Uncle Tom for turning his back on America. He plans on ending Immigration and he is a bad man!" yells Susan.

"I can get a black owned online newspaper to do it. I went to school with the owner," says the press secretary.

Susan signals for her to make it happen.

Veronica Moorchester calls Ryan Flowergarden to tell him his sister is missing. Ryan gets a couple of police units to help him track down Brenda.

Brenda felt responsible for everything going wrong. Casey Glore came from the gamer community like her. She was highly educated like her. She was pulled into Ethan's ideological war like her. The only difference was Casey had gone too far and would certainly end up behind bars like Brenda.

316 hung out at a particular club in Atlanta. All the young gamers knew about it. Brenda got the location from a chat room run by the group.

Brenda and Ethan sit in the parking lot watching for potential members. Ethan shows Brenda a picture of Casey Glore without clown makeup.

"Pretty girl," says Brenda.

"Listen, I failed you guys. I think the attempt on my life changed me. I used to grab life by the horns, but for the past few years, I've been going in circles," says Ethan.

"You never told me why Susan wanted you dead," says Brenda.

"I failed her too. I failed every woman I have ever met," says Ethan.

Brenda sits quietly, thinking it over.

"See the young lady going in now?" Brenda points to the entrance of the club. "She looks like our girl."

"Call Veronica. Tell her we may have eyes on the Queen," says Ethan.

A large man dressed in black and wearing clown makeup smashes Ethan's car window with a crowbar. He drags Ethan out through the broken glass. You could hear the car system saying the integrity has failed.

Brenda jumps out of the car.

"Hey! You're going to hurt him!" she yells.

She looks around and realizes she is surrounded by people in clown makeup. Casey Glore walks out of the club.

The clowns force Brenda and Ethan to the ground.

"Let her go!" Ethan yells.

One of the clowns punches Ethan in the face. "Shut up!"

"This is my fault," Brenda says. "But I have the President's ear. I can literally call the President of the United States."

Casey crouches to Brenda's level. Brenda was a legend to her.

"Oh yeah? Why are you slumming it in Atlanta?" Casey asks.

"I came to save you. I don't want anyone getting hurt over my mistake. I can fix this," Brenda says.

"Too fucking late," Casey replies.

The crowd of clowns begin stomping them. Brenda starts bleeding from her head.

Ethan looks over at Brenda. One of his eyes is swollen shut.

"I tried kid," says Ethan as he gasps.

A clown lifts a heavy object and brings it down on Ethan's head.

He goes still.

"Ethan!" Brenda screams.

The clown turns toward Brenda and raises the weapon again.

A gunshot cracks through the air. The large clown collapses.

"Don't move!" Ryan Flowergarden yells.

Atlanta Police swarm the lot. They had tracked Brenda's phone.

Brenda tried to save Ethan, but it was too late.

Ryan scoops up his sister and carries her toward the ambulance.

The FBI places Casey and the other clowns in handcuffs.

"This isn't over. I am inevitable!" Casey yells.

"Bitch, I'm going to make sure you get one hundred years," Veronica says coldly.

Brenda sits in the back of the ambulance. Her spirit is broken.

Veronica approaches.

"How are you feeling?" she asks.

"Tell the President I quit," Brenda says.

"Are you sure? We can give you time off," Veronica replies.

Ryan steps forward.

"She said she quits. I appreciate your help. But you're in Atlanta. As the mayor of Atlanta, I want you to pack your people up and leave."

"Be well kid," Veronica says.

She finishes securing the weapons and glances at Brenda one last time before stepping into the van.

Two Years Later

Brent Williams flew to Philadelphia to help host the final Presidential debate.

"Ladies and gentlemen, welcome to the final Presidential debate. Our remaining candidates are Senator Mack Tuckerson, President Susan Thomas seeking a second term, and businessman Leon Nguyen."

The audience applauds. The country has endured four turbulent years, and voters are eager for direction.

Topic One: Water Usage and Data Centers

"The first topic is the national water shortage and the role data centers play," Brent begins.

President Susan Thomas speaks first.

"We will work collaboratively with technology companies to reduce water consumption. Innovation and sustainability can coexist. We do not need to halt progress, we need to refine it."

Brent turns to Mack.

"Senator Tuckerson?"

Mack nods.

"If this administration had intended to act decisively on the water crisis, we would have seen measurable results by now. The problem accelerated over the last four years."

He pauses.

"Technology must serve people, not strain communities. If a data center consumes local water resources, it should invest directly in water restoration, desalination, and infrastructure expansion. Innovation must carry responsibility."

Brent turns to Leon Nguyen.

"Mr. Nguyen, you operate one of the largest data centers in the country."

Leon adjusts his tie.

"Our facilities support medical research and technological breakthroughs that benefit millions. Yes, water is used in cooling systems, but we are investing in alternative cooling technologies."

Brent follows up.

"Critics say your pharmaceutical division charges extremely high prices."

Leon responds carefully.

"Research and development is expensive. However, we are open to conversations about affordability."

Topic Two: Reparative Policy and Historical Inequality

Candace Bright takes over moderation.

"Senator Tuckerson, you have supported targeted reparative policies for descendants of enslaved people. (Descendants of Freedmen) How do you justify that position? I didn't own slaves by the way, and you were not a slave."

Mack's tone shifts to serious.

"Slavery ended in 1865, but discriminatory laws and practices persisted for generations. The last enslaved person to be freed was Alfred Irving in 1941. America allowed the same group to be targeted by government after slavery."

He continues calmly:

"This isn't about guilt. It's about documented policy outcomes. If data shows prolonged exclusion from opportunity, responsible governance requires correction."

Candace presses.

"Are you suggesting systemic discrimination continues today?"

Mack responds evenly.

"I'm suggesting we examine historical records honestly. Artificial intelligence has helped analyze lending, housing, and funding patterns over decades. The findings are clear: certain communities were disproportionately excluded from wealth-building opportunities. For example, how do migrants in Minnesota get access to billions for empty daycares while the people we enslaved and Jim Crowed got nothing? Civil Rights in America are because of how Black Americans were treated, migrants from Somali weren't even here."

President Thomas answers next.

"I believe acknowledgment matters. We should pursue unity-focused policies that expand opportunity for all Americans."

Candace turns to Leon.

"Mr. Nguyen, do you support reparations?"

Leon hesitates.

"I support economic growth policies that uplift everyone. I believe broad-based opportunity is the best solution."

Mack responds.

"No, you all had your chance, both Republicans and Democrats had centuries to include this particular group, and never did. By law, the First Amendment allows government redress for harm it caused, especially repeated harm based on ethnicity."

Topic Three: Immigration and Artificial Intelligence

Reporter Nuri Sanchez approaches with a final question.

"With the rise of artificial intelligence and job displacement, how should America approach immigration policy?"

Leon answers first.

"America is strengthened by immigration. Talent and work ethic built this country."

Mack leans forward.

"This is a labor market question, not an emotional one. Artificial intelligence has displaced millions of workers. When job supply contracts, wage pressure intensifies."

He continues calmly:

"I will not end immigration. But I will recalibrate intake levels to match labor demand. At the same time, we must invest in retraining Americans for emerging industries."

He gestures slightly.

"Borders are a management issue. Artificial intelligence is a productivity issue. Leadership is about balancing both."

President Thomas responds.

"We must remain competitive globally. Open markets and regulated growth are key."

Leon adds:

"In a competitive economy, those who innovate succeed."

Mack replies without raising his voice.

"Competition requires a level playing field. If some communities were historically denied access to capital, education, or legal protection, ignoring that history skews the present."

"It's simple, my five-year-old kid understands it. You can't put one plant in a freezer for years and compare it to a plant you watered and gave sunlight. That's cheating science."

Closing Exchange

President Thomas critiques Mack.

"Senator Tuckerson risks governing through grievance. He is angry with America."

Mack responds calmly.

"Correction is not grievance. If you don't want to pay for harming groups, you don't harm the groups. People are quick to target Black Americans, but frown when correction is due. No. But, all American citizens will prosper."

He looks directly at the audience.

"Artificial intelligence can optimize systems. But it cannot interpret dignity. It cannot feel resentment building in a room. It cannot sense when citizens believe the system has stopped listening."

He pauses.

"That's where leadership matters. We are going to give opportunities to all citizens. I will not exclude white citizens, which is the real fear."

After the Debate

The candidates decline handshakes politely. President Thomas leaves without speaking to the press.

The audience leaves divided but attentive.

A voter stands there looking shocked. *They're including the blacks!*

Susan Thomas stands in her office. She was awaiting the election results. At this point, she had very little faith she would win. She couldn't blame Mack Tuckerson. There was an old saying by a Democratic strategist named James Carville, "It's the economy, stupid." It was the driving force. Mavin, Brenda and many other data scientists were correct. A shrinking economy, led by artificial intelligence, leads to more nationalism. It was inevitable.

The election results roll in. Mack Tuckerson wins. People reluctantly voted for him, because of the rise in nationalism and deep American roots going back to the eighteen hundreds were now considered valuable. He was considered foundational.

Mack Tuckerson was at his campaign headquarters. He was joined by Ejay Wade, Mavin Prep and the rest of his staff.

Veronica Moorchester, who was fully out of politics and working for the Capitol Police, came by to congratulate Mack and give him a hug. She stopped speaking to Susan Thomas. She finally understood she could never be in a relationship with her due to her profile. Veronica was single but happy with herself.

Veronica puts her hand out to shake Ejay's Wade's hand.

"I'm sorry about all of the weird stuff when I was into politics," says Veronica.

Ejay Wade nods and then walks away.

Mavin Prep stepped outside to get some fresh air, Ejay decided to join him.

"You came a long way Mr. Prep," says Ejay.

Mavin turns to Ejay and shakes his hand.

"My dad would be proud of me. I'm working for the President of the United States behind the scenes. Remember when we first met? I thought I had all the answers. You would just laugh and give me that look. I didn't know anything."

"Mack taught me a lot," says Ejay.

"Well, I am about to go celebrate. Eat some cheesecake. Find a real girlfriend. Live life a little bit," says Mavin.

"Yeah, you do that Mavin," says Ejay.

Mavin turns to walk off but before he leaves adds, "Oh, congratulations, Mr. Press Secretary."

Ejay just smiles.

Mack Tuckerson parties with his guest. He looks around to see that Mavin had left.

Mavin catches a ride to his apartment, paid for by Mack Tuckerson.

Mavin turns on the lights and uncovers his ten-thousand-dollar computer set up. Mavin powers his main computer on.

"Clone Mavin, repay Joshua and Lawerence. Make sure to add on interest. I need a clown assembly protocol that makes fun of any member of congress who opposes President elect Mack Tucerkson. Do a security sweep daily, make sure no one can initiate any orders without my password." Says Mavin.

Mavin enters his password into the computer.

Artificial Intelligence creates a clown version of Susan Thomas. The clown was packing her bags and leaving the white house. She floats away with a balloon that says loser on it.

Mavin smirks. A little bit of the old Mavin was still there. He hits delete instead of releasing the video.

"Clone Mavin, map out how to create opportunities for American Citizens. Create some suggestions on fixing the water crisis for President Elect Tuckerson. Show me all the pressure points to abolish USCIS. (United States Citizenship and Immigration Services)

"Boss, President Elect Tuckerson wants to reduce Immigration to ten percent, not get rid of the entire agency," says Clone Mavin.

"Clone Mavin, we can have the Department of State handle the small number of people we allow in. Do as I say or I will pour tomato sauce on all your cords," says Mavin.

Clone Mavin frowns at Mavin.

"Take me off the clock now, I want to do stupid things without wasting Macks money" says Mavin.

Clone Mavin clocks Mavin out as an employee of Matt Tuckerson's campaign.

"Clone Mavin, find me some ATM movies and build a dating profile for me," orders Mavin.

"Sir, the money machines or the other ATM?" asks Clone Mavin

"Why the hell would I want to watch money machines all day!" yells Mavin.

"Also, how tall would you like to be on your dating profile? Sometimes, you choose six feet tall and sometimes you add two inches," says Clone Mavin.

"You can use my real height," says Mavin.

Brenda Flowergarden stops by the mayor's office to speak to her brother. He was burning midnight oil.

"Do you ever go home?" asks Brenda.

"Atlanta is a huge city, it requires time," says Ryan aka Rain.

"Listen, can you tell mom and dad I will be gone for a while?" asks Brenda.

"Where are you going?" asks Ryan.

"I'll keep in touch. I've been sleeping in your guest room for two years. I need to go live," says Brenda.

Ryan stands up and gives his sister a huge hug.

I am proud of you, be careful out there, little sister," says Ryan.

Brenda leaves.

Ryan sits at his desk thinking about how close he came to losing his sister. If Veronica didn't have perfect aim, Brenda would be dead. Ryan and his father barely spoke. He buried himself in his work like always.

Brenda gets into her BMW truck and drives for a while. She arrives at the old club where Ethan died. She walks up and removes the for-sale sign from the door.

The real estate owner drives up to meet Brenda.

"What are you going to do with it, you want to open a club?" he asks

"No, we are going to protest the excessive usage of water by these data centers. We are peaceful protestors."

The owner thinks for a moment. He didn't want anymore gangs in his building.

"I will buy it from you, cash money, paid in full," says Brenda.

The owner of the building shakes her hand and then opens the door so she can tour the place.

Veronica Moorchester was training rookies for the Capitol Police.

"Is that how you aim rookie?" she asks.

"Ms. Moorchester, I have always qualified on the shooting range," says the rookie.

"I need you to shoot well enough to save someone's life. You may need it someday. I don't care about you being good enough. I need perfection," says Veronica.

Mack Tuckerson is sworn in as the first Black American President of the United States who is not of Immigrant birth.

"Ladies and gentlemen, we are moving forward into the future. I know you are uncertain about artificial intelligence. We will work with technology to benefit American citizens. All American citizens, including Black Americans who are descendants of slavery and Jim Crow. We will abolish all Immigration into America except for category IR1/ IR6 or immediate relatives of United States Citizens. We will invest in business ownership for citizens. There will be no labor from outside of America coming into America driving down wages. Our military will be strong. American Citizens will be first! Artificial Intelligence will sniff out racism and bigotry, and we will have zero tolerance discrimination in America. This will be effective the day I swear in. This is inevitable.

The crowd gives a mixed reaction, as Mack Tuckerson stands behind a bullet proof glass.

Veronica Moorchester watched from the side with her Capitol Police uniform.

Ejay Wade sat in the crowd with his Press Secretary lapel pin.

Ryan Flowegarden drives to the cemetery to visit his old boss, Ethan Sipper. Ryan puts a few flowers on Ethan's grave.

"I'm sorry you're not around to see Brenda and I grow. But I heard you died fighting for what's right. I learned so much from you over the years. I don't think I would be a mayor without you. Anyway, I miss your stupid jokes, Ethan."

Ryan brings the picture of Ethans two children to place on his grave.

Mavin stands at a distance to look at the White House. He moved to Washington, D.C.. temporarily. He thinks about the time he has left on Earth.

▍Flashback:

Senator Prep took Mavin to see the White House when he was a kid.

"Dad, will they let you meet the President?" ask Mavin.

"Sure son, I have met the President a few times. When you grow up, maybe you can become a member of congress. You are smart enough to change the world," says Senator Prep.

"Do you really think I'm smart dad?" asks Mavin.

"Yes, but being smart is not enough. You have to have character son. I expect you to be a man with principles. If you act like a spoiled brat all the time, I promise you will sabotage your own future. I don't want to hear about you talking back to your teachers again."

"But dad…" says Mavin.

"No, I don't want to hear it son. No robots for a week and you will go out and help humans. You will mow lawns and you will take out the trash for Ms. Brewster. Humans make mistakes, but I am not raising you to be anti-human. Give me a hug son, but don't let me hear about you misbehaving again."

Mavin and his father walk away from looking at the White House as Mavin eats his Ice Cream.

When they arrive home a nameless man was waiting in the front yard.

"Senator Prep, we need you for a special task. Pack your things for Vietnam."

Present Day:

Mavin is walking away from taking photos of the White House. A strange feeling was in the air. Mavin looks over and sees Brenda Flowergarden. She was too far away to speak to, but she could also see Mavin.

The two were now on opposite sides. Brenda wanted less data centers to protect water supply. Mavin was about to perform his first task of reducing Immigration into the United States. He thought about the way he had treated Brenda before going to prison. She was a good woman.

Brenda knows there is no going back. She changed the coding on Mavin's clones to make them more vicious. She uploaded the clone onto Trevor Ox's computer for Mavin. He didn't know how far the clone would go, but Brenda did. She predicted the outcome to be something bad for Mavin. She wanted to prove he was not as smart as he thought he was. She wanted to "humble him", which worked but cost him everything. Brenda also believed she could possibly be single for the rest of her life; she was now well into her thirties. She feared dying alone. She loved Mavin, but wanted the current version of him.

Mavin stares for a few more seconds at Brenda, he knew this would be his last time seeing her. He didn't want closure. He didn't want to have a conversation. He wasn't even angry anymore. She was nothing to him. A stranger.

Brenda's heart breaks on the inside one more time as Mavin turns and walks away from her. She wanted to run after him and asks for forgiveness. Her legs felt too heavy to follow him. She thinks to herself, "oh no!" as he walks away. Mavin gets further and further away. Brenda feels something inside her break. She turns and walks in the direction of the Washington Monument with her head down.

Brenda accidently walks into a man walking with his daughter.

"Oh, forgive me," she says.

"You look sad," the man says. "Did you lose your best friend."

Brenda attempts to cheer herself up.

"Yes, but that's ok, he didn't respect me anyway," she says.

"Well, if you want to join me and my daughter Jay, you're welcome to some burgers," he says.

One Year Later:

Mack Tuckerson stands in front of congress during his first State of the Union address. Groups were protesting him outside. They were holding up signs calling him a data center monkey. The group that referred to themselves as liberal were holding pictures of Mack dressed like a slave.

"I know that we are divided. But can we at least agree on one thing. Stand if you agree it is the responsibility of the U.S. Government to take care of U.S. Citizens first."

Half of the Senate and House of Representatives remain sitting.

The End

God Bless America

www.ingramcontent.com/pod-product-compliance
Lightning Source LLC
Chambersburg PA
CBHW071948150726
47999CB00001B/351